DUST

DUST

MARK THOMPSON

RedDoor

Published by RedDoor

www.reddoorpublishing.com

© 2016 Mark Thompson

ISBN 978-1-910453-22-3

A CIP catalogue record for this book is available from the British Library

Cover design: Liron Gilenberg www.ironicitalics.com

Typesetting: www.typesetter.org.uk

Printed and bound in Great Britain by Clays Ltd, St Ives plc.

For my mother and father – the best parents any child could have wished for and with special thanks to Steve Jones, Robert Middleton, John Gill and Sandy Farmer for inspiration, friendship and unfailing belief.

With limitless love to my family – Liz, Claudia, Izzy and Nathaniel Green for making this and everything else in life, so incredibly wonderful.

Prologue

If there's one thing in life that should be considered, I guess it's the idea that we all face a test. At some point. Maybe early or maybe late. Or somewhere in the middle. Who knows where or when? I mean, can you think of one solitary person who has rolled through life without a test of some sort? And I don't mean school exams, or not running screaming from the dentist's chair or having your appendix out. I mean something bigger and deeper than all these things. I mean, look at Old Man Taylor, for instance. He's had his test. He didn't bank on it, but he had it. But I'll come to that...

– ONE –

It was a perfect summer day as El Greco and I lay on our backs in the rough grass at the edge of the sports field, out back of the old brick locker rooms, gazing at billowing puffs of pure white cloud in the rich blue sky, spotting shapes.

I told him I could see Mount Rushmore, and I could, I swear.

He pointed to the plume of cotton wool that vanished slowly in its margins as I stared upwards and said, 'Yeah, sure looks like it. There's Jefferson, Lincoln and Washington, and who's that other guy? Roosevelt.'

I marvelled at his knowledge for a second or two and said, 'Oh, yeah, I forgot about him,' like I knew.

El Greco was the smartest kid I ever met. He was a sage.

He was ten years old.

We lay on our backs for what seemed like an eternity and guessed at shapes while the sun beat down and the long dry grass shimmered in the faintest zephyr of a breeze. Crimson tissue poppies bobbed back and forth with the motion of well-wishers waving handkerchiefs on a distant railroad station. We blew smoke rings as we drew on cigarettes. If we bought cigarettes, we bought Kents. My father smoked Kents, so did El Greco's mom, so if we were caught we could say we found them in the car and were just bringing them in. We also stole cigarettes from our folks.

3

'Wouldn't it be great if they came in banana flavour?' I said, as El Greco watched a perfectly formed ring lose its shape and drift upwards until it emulated the buckled wheel of some abandoned bicycle. He sat up suddenly and pushed his hand through the ring, smoke gathering momentarily around his wrist. I felt a sudden sadness for its loss.

He turned to face me, brows knitted in consideration. He smiled, nodding. Slowly at first, then rapidly as enthusiasm overtook him. 'Yeah, you got something there.' He nodded again. 'Imagine that? Chocolate cigarettes. Wow.'

I warmed to the theme, basking in the limelight. 'Strawberry and vanilla, pistachio, tutti-frutti!' I yelled, carried away.

'Yeah, you've definitely hit on something there,' he said dreamily, rolling back in the dry grass.

We each used our cigarettes to start tiny fires, watching intently as faint fingers of orange flame licked like tiny gaudy snakes up a yellow stem, suddenly leaping to its neighbour, and then as quickly to its neighbour's neighbour, until smoke was billowing white and grey and flashed with orange as our panicking boots stamped it all into the hard brown earth. The smell of smoke was everywhere as dust and pollen rose like diesel fumes from an old truck just started; we coughed hard as the acrid mixture filled our lungs and clung to our hair.

'There'll be hell to pay if my mom smells smoke on me,' I rasped, as we kicked over the traces of dirt and ash.

'Come on, let's go get some soda or something, it's time to get home anyways,' El Greco said, spitting on the blackened ground. We drank soda, my particular buzz being root beer, but sometimes we drank coffee, just to be different. It marked us out. It made old folks jitter. It was part of our plan.

4

We stuffed our hands in the pockets of our jeans and jogged across the field. El Greco did his imitation of Bugs Bunny, which always made me laugh, but killed me then because he was wearing his Looney Tunes T-shirt with Bugs on the front. 'What's Up, Doc?' I mimicked. I couldn't do it like he could, but I could do a great rendition of Mickey Mouse shouting 'Pluto!' so I did that too and El Greco laughed like hell. God, he made me happy. He knew all the right things to say, and just when to say them. For a ten-year-old he was one hell of a guy.

We stopped at the top of the field to sword-fight with green twigs we snapped from a willow tree. I was King Arthur and he was Errol Flynn as Captain Kidd. We crossed the roadway into Mister Jeb Doughty's wheat field, passing the broken-down barn that defied wind and rain and always stood half-gone but resolute, despite time and the seasons' relentless assaults of thigh-deep snow and scorching sun. Heading back towards El Greco's house, we heard the distant wail of sirens. We walked back to the fence, hoping to see what all the fuss was about.

There they were, racing up the rise.

We clambered on to the fence to get a better view. Two huge red fire trucks hurtled towards us with sirens blaring and lights flashing like the waltzers we loved to ride whenever Butler's Funfair hit town.

We watched with fixed eyes as dust flew into the air from the sun-baked road.

'Where do you think they're going?'

'Must be a house fire someplace, or Fatty Conway got stuck in the courthouse railings again.'

As the pink dust settled I opened my eyes looking east to see where the trucks were headed. There was a fire all right. A big one. Smoke the colour of an old man's hair pumped up to the sky like whipped cream from the far side of the field.

El Greco saw it as I did, and for once he didn't have to spell it out for me.

'Fuck! Get the hell out of here!'

We hit the ground before my words were done, running as fast as we could across the field. We cursed a lot like ten-year-old boys do, but I outdid my record, gasping, 'Fuck! Fuck! Fuck! Fuck! Fuck!' as we ran. The hollow stems of grass whipped our legs, making them smart. We ran until we were breathless, and collapsed in the shade of a blackthorn tree. I almost didn't dare to look back at the sports field, but fear and curiosity got the better of me and I turned my head. The sky, which had been perfect blue with tufted clouds, was grey-white with huge flashing tongues that leaped into the air. In a few brief minutes, fields of play had turned into a war zone. My heart stopped in sympathy with my breathing as I stared incredulously at the scene before me. I thought El Greco could hear the roaring in my heaving chest. I held my breath in the hope that I could slow my heartbeat down. I once saw a movie where somebody injected this guy with adrenaline or curare or something like that which made his heart race so fast he had a heart attack and dropped dead on an airport escalator. Everybody was fooled by it, except me and the detective who solved the case. I felt like I'd been jabbed too.

'Jesus H. Christ! That's one hell of a fire!' El Greco whistled, and thumped the grassy earth where we lay. When a crisis loomed, he had a habit of sounding like an old man who'd seen it all.

'Let's get the fuck out of here,' I said in a low voice.

'Yeah, let's go, the cops just showed up.'

El Greco's calm tones did nothing to slow the waves of panic that had grown to breakers inside my guts. I felt a hand on my shoulder, jumped like a gerbil and spun around to see El Greco grinning at me. 'Come on,' he said confidently, 'no one knows it was us, and besides, it was just an accident.'

His calm flowed through his fingertips and down my shoulder into my arm. I felt the fear subside for a moment, but as he took his hand away and started to walk, crouched down to avoid detection, it flowed back through me. We'd done it this time. We'd done all manner of crazy things and got away with them, but this was different – this was a crime, and the cops were there, larger than life in their black and white Dodge with the dented fenders and gold badges on the doors.

I prayed to a God I didn't truly believe existed for one last chance. I swore I'd be good forever if only he would take me back a few hours in time so that I could put the book of matches back in the barbecue bin where I found them.

No chance. I looked at the spiralling cloud of smoke and muttered, 'Thanks a bunch!'

El Greco was some ways off, keeping low, so I shuffled faster to catch him up. I wasn't going to be left out on my own in case the cops spied me.

I ditched the matchbook in Horse River, which was nearly dead dry, just a lazy trickle left to mark it on the map. We had not seen rain for what seemed like forever. I tried to look easy as I caught up with him, and, sensing me there, El Greco straightened up and stuffed his hands in his pockets. He grabbed a piece of wheat stem, stuck it between his teeth, and chewed it as though he didn't give a damn for anything, and just for a second I didn't either.

I sighed and said, 'It's only a load of old dry grass anyways. I bet anything could have started that fire. Remember what my old man said that time about the burning bush, and how God put a holy spirit into that bush in the middle of nowhere and it just set itself on fire? I just bet that's what happened here!'

There I was, seeking revenge on God because he hadn't taken me back a few hours so I could put the maniac matches back. Served him right as far as I was concerned. If he ever needed a favour from me he could just go to hell, and that was the end of that. Forgiveness wasn't a strong suit with me. If there was a God, which I truly doubted, he had had his opportunity to make my life a whole lot sweeter, and he'd just blown it.

I started to feel less guilty about opening the little envelopes my father gave me to take to Sunday school, and removing what I liked to regard as a fair percentage, which I split with El Greco and spent on candy and cigarettes.

Of course Mister Schwartz didn't actually sell me cigarettes. He just sold me candy and I fed quarters into the machine at the side of his store to buy the cigarettes, which I stuffed inside my underwear to prevent detection by my ever-vigilant and pious brother, Adolf.

Of course his name wasn't really Adolf. It was Cecil. My mother named him after Cecil B. DeMille. I tried to like him. It was an uphill task but I persevered. He could be almost likeable sometimes, but he was a thorn in my side and he treated my mother like trash. My father indulged him because he saw Super Bowl stardom at the end of the rainbow. They were both sports nuts. My grandfather had fought in France in World War Two, and he said that if Cecil had been around then that war would have been four years shorter. He said that thousands of lives could have been spared, or else all of Europe would now be talking

8

German and driving Volkswagens, depending which side Cecil had been on.

I jumped suddenly from thoughts of God and guilt when I heard the police siren rise from rest. The fire, escalating in the stiffening breeze, crept steadily forward and fanned towards a small group of dormitory-type homes that made up the Green Valleys Retirement Park. The Green Valleys was a group of one hundred single-bedroom bungalows sited around a shallow pond the planners called the Community Lake. In reality the lake was sixty feet by ninety feet and six inches deep so that the folks with dementia didn't drown as they repelled imaginary pirates they thought were invading from magenta-sailed corsairs. The water was dyed deep blue, the shade only ever seen in vacation brochures for sunny Mexico or 'ocean scent' lavatory cleaner.

'Lie down!' El Greco hissed, flattening himself into the stubble as another police car sped along the roadway through swirling banks of smoke.

I dropped to my belly and stuffed my face down in the sharp tubes of cut wheat, which felt hard as drinking straws sticking in my skin, causing me to curse out loud.

'Keep still, for Jesus' sake, J.J. Do you have to make so much fucking noise?'

El Greco cursed a lot when he wanted to make a point.

'I can't help it, Tony. This stuff is stabbing my eyes out,' I said, hoping exaggeration would win sympathy and let me off the hook.

'Try telling that to your warder when you get to Rikers Island.'

His words filled me with dread, and I felt my throat tighten and a lump the size of an eight-ball rose in the barren gully of my throat.

'Only kidding,' he said with a grin, 'we're okay, the cops have gone out to Green Valleys.'

I dared to raise my head an inch or two and saw the blue and red flashing beacons racing away from us on the Green Valleys road.

'Come on, let's get out of here while we've got the chance to save our skins,' I said, sighing with relief, and feeling suddenly and unexpectedly tired.

'Yeah, let's go,' said El Greco, letting the slightest whisper of quiet release fall into his words.

We stuck to an overgrown path across the field to avoid the stream of excited kids running towards the now massive pall of white smoke, which reminded me of the month of February on our kitchen calendar. *Sierra Nevada, and the ski runs of Mammoth Lakes seen from the gentle town of Bishop, California.*

'Look at all these kids! Jesus, we're for it! Someone will guess it was us, I just know it,' I said dismally, thinking of Cecil, and his certain assumption that every bad deed in our little town was perpetrated by me.

'Right, let's slide in with them and go back down there and take a look,' said El Greco excitedly.

'What the hell for?'

'Because if we don't we'll be the only kids for miles who aren't down at the field, and even someone who isn't too bright may find that just a little odd, don't you think?'

He was right. He was always right.

We fell in behind a group of three kids from the local orphanage. You could always tell the orphanage kids: they seemed to dress about eight years behind the times, as though they were in a piece of newsreel footage about some event that had happened not too long after I was born.

You could also tell the orphanage kids because they stuck together in the way that fox cubs follow their mother everywhere; you always saw two or three younger kids with an older one. That was how you knew they were orphans. My mother once caught me making fun of them to some of my buddies. I knew it was wrong to do it even before she caught me, but I did it just the same. Always playing the fool. My group of admirers giggled like girls when I dropped my shoulders down and bent at the knees, holding my head slightly to one side and lolling it about making goofy noises as though I was not right in the head. Bobby Stockton didn't laugh, he knew how wrong it was, but he said nothing; his look said enough. Bobby believed in God and hell; he often steered me away from stuff that I ought not to be heading towards. If El Greco had been there, he'd have told me to shut the fuck up, too.

'Those children hang their heads because they've got the weight of the world on them, because they don't have a mother or father to love them or nurse them when they're sick, and because they know that you all know they wear hand-me-down clothes. Don't you ever let me catch you making fun of those poor children again, J.J. Walsh.'

Her words stung me like icy hail driven by fierce winds. I had never felt such burning shame, as though the ground would surely split and swallow me in a great black gash, down into the very bowels of the fiery hell at the core of the Earth. I tried a goofy grin for my audience to show them I was smarter than my mother, but they all looked as broken as I felt, and I knew the moment was lost forever. I turned to my mother, and I know I touched her with my honesty when I said that I was real sorry, that I'd never do such a thing again. I meant what I said and she seemed to know it. She placed her hand on my head so gently I cried, burying my face in the soft cotton of her summer dress, hiding my shameful tears from view. I never made fun of them again.

El Greco never mocked them. I guess he was only a whisper away from their misery, his old man being what he was and all.

We tagged along behind the orphans down through the scrub grass and across the shiny road to the top sports field. I felt miserable, recalling the day my mother had put me back in my place, and I was doubly weighed down, not just with guilt at starting the biggest grass fire seen in Cranford County since before I was born, but with the iron-clad certainty that we would be caught and punished and put to shame for the entire town to see. I visualised hateful Mister Barr lecturing our school after morning prayers and the proud anthem, telling them all that two of their contemporaries, J.J. Walsh and Tony Papadakis, had been found guilty of wanton fire-raising and were now awaiting their fate, whatever that might be. I could see the fury in his piggy eyes and the small blue veins, all broken in his red shiny too-close-shaved face. I feared and hated that man in a way he could never have understood.

It occurred to me that there might be a possibility that we could go to the electric chair. I'd only ever seen murderers in movies get the chair for crimes too horrific to contemplate, and I had certainly never seen anyone electrocuted for starting a fire, not even one as big as this, but the thought made me shiver.

I got a whiff of singeing pink and blackened flesh and leaped from my daydream with a strangled cry. 'Not the chair!' I screamed, causing El Greco to jump and the orphans to turn around and stare at me. I grimaced with embarrassment at El Greco, who playfully punched my arm, as though he had read my thoughts. I realised with cool relief that the smell was not my skin frying but the acrid tang of a discarded car tyre belching pungent black smoke.

We stood with a group of gawping children by the side of a fire truck and watched as the fire fighters sprayed gallons of hissing water on to the flames. It seemed to me they were fighting a losing battle, for, as fast as they were advancing into the orange frenzy, so the breeze was blowing life into the flames at the far side of the field, and those flames were getting closer and closer to the neat little houses of the Green Valleys park.

'If it burns down the retirement park, we'll get the chair,' I whispered hurriedly to El Greco.

'Ten-year-old kids don't go to the chair, and they don't go to Rikers either. And besides, if you stay cool there ain't nobody apart from me and you who knows,' he said softly.

He was right. Carl Newton Mahan had been six years old when he killed his friend Cecil Van Hoose, who was eight, over a piece of scrap iron on May 18, 1929 in eastern Kentucky. He took his father's shotgun and shot his little friend and even he didn't get the chair. This was another thing we got from the *Guinness Book of Records*. Everyone thought that because we were ten years old we only thought silly things and played like kids, but we smoked and cursed and did all kinds of shit. We never shot anyone though.

'What if Adolf knows?' I panicked again at the thought that somehow my twelve-year-old sadist of a brother would know what I had done. He had an uncanny knack for finding out my darkest secrets. He would sometimes accuse me of them at get-togethers, when there were plenty of people in earshot, and I would blush like a homecoming queen, the letters 'G-U-I-L-T-Y' appearing in trashy neon lights across my forehead, despite my strangled protestations of innocence. I would fold like a house of cards in front of the district attorney, I just knew it.

I watched transfixed as the flames ate the dry grass in a frenzy, reminding me of a speeded-up section in a colour movie I once saw when an adventurer seeking the lost treasure of an ancient Inca people fell into a swamp and was attacked by piranhas in a mass of bloody boiling water. His last horrific scream was echoing around my head when I heard the fire chief barking commands into his crackling radio. Two more fire trucks swung back to the road, sirens shrieking, bells clanging, rolling from side to side as their drivers fought to control the heavy machines. I watched them gaining speed, hurtling along the normally quiet road towards the retirement park. Groups of dogwood trees and gently swaying poplars hid them for fractions of time, and smoke the colour of clouds swallowed them until they reappeared again as determined as before, big red racing dogs coming out of the traps, chasing a flaming hare.

I started to breathe easier when the flames by the park stopped moving forward. We couldn't see them for smoke, but the firemen had control, heroes every one. A bizarre scenario popped into my head, of dozens of old folks in chequered golf pants and sneakers, and housecoats and curlers, jumping for their lives into the six-inch pool. I imagined them lying on their fronts in the lake with their behinds sticking up from the water. It occurred to me that they'd look like dozens of eggs poaching in a great blue pan. The thought of this caused me to laugh out loud. I suppose it was relief that my nightmare was receding and my chances of going to the electric chair were lessening, but I lost control. I stood by the fire truck shaking with laughter. I folded my arms and wrapped them around my body in an effort to control myself. I bent forward and put my head between my knees but it did no good. Streams of tears rolled down my cheeks, causing brown channels to appear through the fine layer of soot that had attached itself to my suntanned face.

El Greco put his arm around my shoulders and patted my back. He murmured something to me, but I couldn't hear what he said over the noise of the engine. I stood upright and turned my tearstained face to his. The look of alarm in his eyes turned to a ten-foot grin when he realised I was laughing. His teeth were dazzling against his tanned face, and he patted me on the back again and ruffled my hair with his hand, much as my father had done when I hit my first home run in Little League. 'Let's go, every-thing is going to be okay,' he said softly as he turned his head slowly around to check whether anybody was watching us. Nobody was. The fire was diminishing, the way that a pool of methylated spirit does when it burns, shrinking inwards from its circumfer-ence, leaving a telltale ring to show its original size. Some of the teenage kids were starting to drift away, making out they hadn't been as excited as the younger kids, but they had been; they just didn't want it known.

That's the thing about kids. When they're young they are excited by everything around them, but when they get older, twelve or thirteen, they become aware of themselves and how they look, and everything outside of that is just bullshit then.

'Look at them,' I said in my own disgusted way, 'they don't even know a good fire when they see one!'

El Greco shook his head, and nodded in agreement. 'Yeah, they just want to be cool, and they're gonna miss the rest of the fun.'

'What fun?' I asked raising my eyebrows, exaggerating my bemusement.

'Why, when the cops start asking questions, of course.'

He looked me dead in the eye, and I swallowed hard, trying to get a peach pit down a drinking straw.

'Oh, Jesus,' I said quietly.

'Tell you what, let's go down to the cops and tell them we saw two kids about so old, one wearing a Bugs Bunny T-shirt, and we saw them start a fire and as they ran off they said they couldn't give a fart if the old folks fried like barbecue chicken. That should take the heat off of us all right.'

I stared at him with my mouth open like the dead cod at Fulton fish market. He stuck his tongue out at me and rolled his eyes back in his head, laughing. Then he saw the strain in my face, fists clenched by my sides, fingers crunched into my palms all white and purple.

'All right, hotshot,' he said, 'let's go for real this time. We're late anyway.'

We shuffled back towards El Greco's house, filtering along with the meandering stream of soot-stained kids. I had the smell of smoke in my nostrils, and when I sniffed my shirt it had the scent of my father in late fall when he burned dead leaves from the maple trees out the back of our yard.

I tried to edge nearer to the boy in front of me, moving close to sniff his shirt. I tripped over a tree root and fell forward against him, bloodying my nose. He turned around and shoved me backwards. 'Hey! What da hellya doin'?' His voice was hard, clipped, nasal. A boxer's voice. He was from out of town and boy, did he look mean. He was probably three years older than me and much bigger, and I didn't want to fight with him, no way. I didn't want to fight with anybody, but particularly not him. For once I wished that Adolf were with me. He would shred him if that kid tried to push him around. Cecil had fast dukes and he liked to use them. Usually on me.

El Greco jumped to my defence. 'He just tripped, that's all; he's blind in one eye, so he can't see straight. He's always falling over. He's real sorry, aren't you, J.J.?'

This guy was probably from Washington Heights or the Bronx and probably had more fights in one day than I would have in my lifetime. I like to think that he wouldn't have hit me because I was a kid, but, either way, I guess El Greco's lie worked. Even a tough guy from the Bronx wouldn't hit a blind kid.

I sighed deeply and held my throbbing nose as the tough kid paced off, swaggering slightly as he went, letting all the other kids know he'd scored a victory without having to throw a single punch. 'Fucking asshole,' I murmured to myself, getting up, making damned sure he was out of earshot.

'What the hell did you do that for? I thought you were dead for sure!'

'I just fancied getting into training for my real contest against Cassius Clay Saturday week,' I said bitterly, dabbing blood from my nose.

Clay had beaten Sonny Liston twice, once in '64 in seven rounds to take the title from Liston, and again in '65, this time in two minutes twelve seconds. I remembered each fight vividly; particularly the fans yelling 'Fake! Fake! Fake!' as Liston went down in the first round of that second bout.

Nobody would have shouted 'Fake!' if that Bronx boy had put me on the ground. That would have been real enough.

El Greco didn't say anything further. He had saved my skin and I'd given him sour grapes.

'I was trying to see if his shirt smelled of smoke and I tripped,' I said softly, by way of apology.

'Yeah, and you nearly needed Doctor Kesh,' he said giggling to himself. He could never stay mad at me for long, so I laughed too. Doctor Kesh was Armenian and his name was Keshishyan, but that was too difficult to say.

We arrived at El Greco's house, having passed back through Mister Jeb Doughty's field, seeing Jay Baglia sneaking out of the old barn all furtive, until he grinned and waved. We knew he grew pot in there because we hid out there often and saw strange plants growing in a corner where the roof was down and weeds sprouted high. El Greco figured what the taller weeds were, but we never let on. Not to a soul, except Bobby, who came with us to take a look.

We walked around to the back yard to enter by the kitchen door. Nobody under the age of twenty-one was allowed through the front door. It was an unwritten rule and I never broke it; even when rain poured down I always took the long route to the kitchen. The smell of hot charcoal and hickory wood chips charring drifted across the back yard. A welcoming homely smell, redolent of summer evenings and relaxed but excited affairs, when tail-wagging barking dogs gave chase to children playing tag. Any other day I would have breathed the perfumed air, almost able to taste it, but I was somewhat put off by the sight of smoke rising from the vent above the old brick barbecue.

'Late as usual,' said El Greco's mom.

She was pretty. I had no idea how old she was. I never saw a woman since who switched the roles of weary mother-of-two and sex siren as easily as she did. She had a way of smiling as though she knew your innermost thoughts and was relaying them back to you. She made me blush the colour of a distress flare just by smiling that knowing smile, and sometimes I felt like saying out loud, 'I wasn't thinking that!', such was my guilt. Even though I didn't really believe she could read my mind, in truth deep down I had just the sneaking fear that she could. Too much religion and the threat of eternal damnation were weights around me, and, like most who try, I was never fully able to cut those chains.

Missus Papadakis's patterned sleeveless sundress boasted summer flowers and poppies in scarlet, green and yellow on ice-cream white. The loops were empty where a matching belt should have exaggerated her slim waist but she knew it wasn't needed. Her figure never changed, but sometimes she looked nineteen, and then she was older than time itself. I guess the way she held herself told a story of how she was inside. Some days it was as though the weariness of life itself had feasted and sucked the very soul from her; an instant later she would radiate a sexuality that made me embarrassed to look her up and down – though I still did when I thought she wasn't paying attention to me.

I saw her nearly naked once. It was the day after El Greco and I had been looking through her Sears mail order catalogues. We found them in the bureau drawer one hot July day when his folks were out and we were searching the house for cigarettes. We were looking at guitars and bicycles at first then came across the lingerie section. Pages and pages of women modelling underwear. We gawped at them, and in some shots we could actually see the outlines of dark nipples and hairy bushes through the almost transparent material. We spent hours staring at them and getting all hot under the collar. If we heard a car pull up or a door shut somewhere

19

we would slam the catalogues shut and stuff them back in the bureau, red-faced from guilt and passion. After that first discovery, we would spend hours looking at those photographs every chance we got when the house was empty. Busty women in basques and French knickers and stockings and silk pyjamas. So real we could almost feel them, stirring things deep within. Anyways, the very next morning after we first discovered the pictures I called for El Greco early, and, after his mom had made us breakfast of maple syrup pancakes, I went up to the bathroom, and through the part-open door to her bedroom I saw her, reflected side-on in a dressing-table mirror, breasts naked, rolling a stocking up her slim tanned leg to the untanned upper thigh where she clipped it to a black garter belt, stark against her milky skin. I froze, fascinated, eyes glazed and staring. Then she turned slightly and caught sight of me. She wasn't mad, she just smiled her smile and said, 'Show's over, J.J.,' then she pushed the door slowly closed with her foot, still smiling. I ran downstairs, face burning, and took my place back at the table, afraid to let on. Missus Papadakis came down a couple of minutes later, acting for all the world as though nothing ever happened.

I never told El Greco. It didn't seem right to, somehow. She never made mention of that day, but whenever she caught me gazing at her in that way she would give me a knowing smile, and I would cough and ask her a pointless question or wander into the back yard whistling any old tune I could summon into my head.

Sometimes she would rest her elbows on the open window frame and stare absently into the back yard, blowing cigarette smoke. I tried to imagine what she was thinking, but I couldn't begin to guess. I never had the nerve to ask. I was afraid to in case I hated what she might say, and would want to go back in time and withdraw my question, which I knew was impossible.

Early in life, my grandfather told me that only three things were certain: birth, death and time. And time only ticked one way: it went forward and never back. It came to be a recurring wish with me, the desire to turn back the clock, to undo what I had done. Always wishing for the impossible, my feet stuck firm in the molasses of the present, unable to shrug off decisions I had made and their unforeseen or disregarded consequences.

I came to recognise a difference between El Greco and me that rotated around guilt, self-belief, and having the courage of conviction. He had a clear and clean understanding of himself and his destiny, where he was going, or rather, where life and destiny were taking him. I always saw my destiny through a fruit jar full of muddied water; distorted and unclear, with nothing truly invisible but nothing fully revealed.

I barely looked at Missus Papadakis as she spoke to us. I was still thinking of the wispy lines of smoke sneaking their silent way out of the brick chimney in the yard.

'There was a big grass fire at the top sports field, so we went over to watch,' said El Greco disingenuously. I swore he had a heart of glass when he added, 'What's to eat?' as though eating was the only thing on his mind.

'Chicken and steak. You boys go and wash up, then you can help me. Your father had to go out,' she said in her hundred-years voice.

'Business?' asked El Greco.

'Business as usual. Business always comes first. Now get on with you. That includes you too, J.J.,' she added, when she noticed that I was still standing by the door, staring at the barbecue as though I had seen it somewhere before but couldn't quite remember where.

I jumped to it and followed El Greco to the bathroom. It had been one hell of a day and I was struggling to keep up the front that El Greco seemed to wear with ease. He appeared to relish being on the edge of something dangerous, in the way that Audie Murphy held onto grenades almost too long in *To Hell and Back*. El Greco always had me on the edge of my seat.

I washed my hands and put them up to my nose, checking for the harsh odour of nicotine. I sighed real hard and splashed cold water in my face, drying it with a towel from a ring by the washstand. I folded the blackened towel almost as neatly as I had found it, and returned it to the ring.

I strolled downstairs after El Greco and tried to work up an appetite by thinking of ice-cream and candy bars. It was a method I often used when I knew I was guilty of something. Parents always seemed to gauge the wellbeing of their kids by the amount they ate. If you couldn't eat at all you were sick or guilty. In my case, my mom would worry that I was sick, but my pop invariably figured I was guilty. He was usually right, so I always tried to eat something, despite the fact that I felt like chucking up. I was not the smartest kid in town but I picked up some things real quick. Being quizzed by the equivalent of the Spanish Inquisition – my father and Adolf – was an experience that taught you to sink or swim. And I was definitely a swimmer. Some days I just needed to float, others I had to tread water, and on bad days I had to do twenty lengths in rough water. I was a swimmer, all right.

'Do you want me to wash the dishes?' I asked Missus Papadakis, trying to feign normality.

'In this household we normally wash the dishes after we've eaten off them, J.J., not before.'

I felt foolish and I looked at her sheepishly so she threw off

22

eighty years and smiled. 'Go on out in the yard and shoot some baskets.' She ruffled my hair and I smiled back at her, blushing red as I sauntered out to the back yard.

El Greco threw the ball so hard it stung my palms, and I threw it back to him as he rushed in towards the basket. We knew this move inside out. He lobbed the ball high in the air with an arcing flick of his arm as he turned his back to the basket. I watched the ball as it rose towards the backboard. An invisible string seemed to pull back on it, slowing it to a pace that suggested it would never reach its target, and then, just as it seemed it would fall to earth, the ball landed softly on the metal rim, clung for a slow second, then rolled around the inside edge and fell through the net to a cheer from El Greco. 'Way to go!' His shout crashed through the quiet of late afternoon like a train bursting from a tunnel, whistle blowing fit to bust.

I wasn't really in the mood for basketball, having so recently been a party to the biggest arson since Watts had exploded three years earlier and Los Angeles saw smoke for five days. Even though I was just seven going on eight, I had sat in front of the television fascinated by the spectacle of rioting people looting shops while buildings burned and soot-streaked policemen fired buckshot at them. There was anger and mayhem and smoke and death. El Greco had said he guessed the policemen understood the anger of the people better than the politicians. He said the policemen knew the people didn't have a chance from birth, and that the politicians were too busy getting re-elected to worry about whether the people had a chance or not.

I sometimes wished he would stop reading *The New York Times* and the *Washington Post*. He used to read them down at the store while Mister Schwartz talked to him about the things that Mister

Schwartz thought were important, like the war in Vietnam and the price of gum. I tried reading them too, but there was too much print and not enough comic strips. I couldn't understand too much of it. El Greco spent hours in there some days. Mister Schwartz said he couldn't wait until Tony Papadakis was old enough to get a job, so that he could actually buy *The New York Times*. Mister Schwartz thought he was a real comedian.

I thought *The New York Times* was a pretty stupid paper. They had blamed the start of the Watts riots on a twenty-one-year-old black man arrested for driving drunk. Marquette Frye. They blamed him for it, but I wasn't falling for that. He couldn't have started anything. I'd seen drunk people and they weren't fit for much. I lost a lot of respect for people who read *The New York Times* after that.

Missus Papadakis came out into the yard with a tray of steak and chicken. She let us drop the meat on to the hot grill and the air was suddenly filled with the spice of hickory and mesquite. The scent of that heady perfume was almost magical, the cologne of back-yard America.

El Greco made up jokes and we laughed and I teased Katherine, his little sister. She had been in her room playing Beatles songs until Missus Papadakis called her down to eat. I said that the Beatles were all right for little girls. She punched me in the guts and winded me bad. She packed a punch for a little kid. I made out I was fooling around, but she still hit me hard. Rocky Marciano would have been proud of that punch, but I couldn't admit to El Greco that his eight-year-old sister had got the better of me. When I got my breath back I stayed rolling on the grass, then sprang up like a jack-in-the-box and pulled a goofy face at Katherine.

She twisted her face back at me. 'I got you good and you know it!'

'Oh, sure!' I shot back in my best sarcastic tone, then picked up a piece of chicken leg and took a bite to make my point. I took another bite and tapped her head with the bone. She laughed. I always teased her, but she liked me all the same. I liked her too. She was pretty neat for a little kid. I didn't tell El Greco that I liked her. He always said she was a pain in the ass, and that she couldn't hang out with us because she was a few years younger than us. But he liked her too.

I drank in the tranquillised calm of early evening in the yard, where the sweet smoke mingled with the scent of pines and eucalyptus in the air, and time slid by unnoticed and silent.

'Time you were heading home, J.J. – your mom will be wondering where you got to,' said Missus Papadakis softly.

'Oh, Mom, just ten minutes more, we want to shoot some baskets,' pleaded El Greco, buying me time. He knew I would want to go home as late as possible, that I didn't fancy my chances with the Spanish Inquisition, even though they had no cause to link me to the fire.

'Plenty of time for that tomorrow, Tony, you know the rules.' Missus Papadakis turned to me and said, 'Say hi to your mom, J.J.'

I recognised that finality, and said that I would. I thanked her for having me to dinner, and said goodbye to El Greco and Katherine. El Greco said, 'Way to go, kid,' and winked at me, turning his back to shield us from his mother's view as he made our secret sign. The first finger of his left hand flat against the side of his nose, followed by the first finger of his right hand drawn in an arc across his forehead. We had that so pat that nobody ever noticed. One time Adolf caught an impression of something

25

between us, but he didn't know what. When he quizzed us, we just looked at him as though he was an alien from *The Twilight Zone* and looked at each other as though to say, *What's his problem?* He's not that dumb, though – he knew something was going on, and most likely added it to his list of things for the big interrogation when he got me stretched on the rack. I feared the day.

El Greco grinned at me with smug pride and I grinned back. I raised my thumb in salute and wandered across the yard to the gate, whistling as I walked. The latch clicked metal on metal as I opened the gate. I waved without looking back and called goodnight as I pulled it behind me.

I swaggered along the road from El Greco's with my thumbs hooked through the belt loops of my jeans, kicking the rubber edge of my baseball boots against the hubcaps of a tatty Ford with airless white-wall tyres that squatted on the grass verge outside Old Man Taylor's house.

Old Man Taylor was a pallbearer for Mister Jennings, the undertaker. He was a scruffy hulk of a man. His wife had died before I was born and my mom said he took the job with the funeral parlour just to be close to the dead. She said he wanted to be nearer to his wife, and I guess he passed messages to her as he helped the departed on their way. He probably said, 'Say hi to Joan for me,' as he used his great calm strength to lift their boxes of pine or oak on to the brass rails in the back of the hearse.

I looked up as I passed the house and I saw Old Man Taylor emptying garbage into his trashcan. His driveway sprouted more varieties of weeds than Yellowstone National Park, and the timber-frame house, which had once been glittering white, was a sad peeling mixture of grey and mint, where old wood and moss

26

meshed together. The outside of the house matched his skin. I had no idea how old he was, but El Greco and I had named him Old Man Taylor after some guy in a western where some gunslingers crossing land were told by some anxious young kid working on fixing a broken fence that they'd have to go around as the owner didn't take too kindly to strangers trespassing on his ranch. One of the gunslingers sat on his horse chewing a matchstick. He gently spat out the pulped wood and asked the kid, all kindly-sounding and reasonable, who the owner was, and the kid said, 'This is Old Man Taylor's ranch, sir.' The gunslinger said, still sounding just as pleasant as all hell, 'Well, son, could you maybe do me a small kindness and pass a message to Mister Taylor for me, and my friends here?' The kid, all smiles now because it looked like they were being real nice and all, said, 'Yes, sir, I surely can, sir.' Then the gunslinger just shot the kid where he stood.

Some nice people you get in westerns.

Old Man Taylor had once been a college footballer. He had arms like artillery shells and a head the size of a basketball. Iron-grey hair bushed out in great waves of steel wire. It was receding now, but he still had plenty. He had the heaviest, most luxuriant moustache I ever saw, grey as his hair. It gave him a mournful look that matched his eyes. He said 'howdy' to anyone who waved as they passed, and he always had a big bag of candy at Hallowe'en, from which he gave handfuls to all the kids who called.

Old Man Taylor loved children. Although he and Joan had two boys, they were grown and gone. His elder son lived somewhere in Europe and said he was just too busy to make it home for his mother's funeral, so Old Man Taylor swore to never speak to the boy again. Old Man Taylor always kept his word. His youngest boy had had a promising career as a marine biologist until he went to Mexico on a field study of the Baja coast and came back into San Diego with a couple of Blue Sharks stuffed to the gills with Acapulco Gold. Customs officers were waiting for his boat when it docked. He faced fifteen years to life for importation of narcotics but did a deal with the district attorney's office for five. He received his sentence and gave evidence against the men who had seduced him with promises of untold wealth and played on his greedy nature. Old Man Taylor said he was the image of his grandfather who had raised Old Man Taylor the hard way on a diet of false promises and failed racetrack certainties. 'Always chasing the rainbow like my fool dad,' was how he described his youngest boy. Old Man Taylor said the kid had made his bed and ought to lie in it so refused him money to hire a lawyer, saying that he was obviously guilty as hell and had no cause to expect anything grander than the San Diego public defender.

After his son gave evidence against the men who financed his trip, Old Man Taylor's boy saw how unfair life could be. Smart lawyers from Los Angeles drew him as the brains and their clients as the victims of his scam. His evidence counted for nothing. The jurors sneered at him when their foreman called their verdicts. What little nerve the boy possessed was frayed to pulp when a tattooed veteran of the California State Penitentiary shoved a playing card into the chest pocket of his prison shirt, slapping him playfully across the head. He showed a mass of gold-capped teeth, grinning as Old Man Taylor's boy took the card out to look at it. The card was a Joker, to which somebody had lovingly added a little extra detail. The Joker had his throat cut. Crimson blood flowed from the gaping gash where his Adam's apple should have been.

I pretended to be out of earshot when my pop told my uncle Sammy all about it one day when they were making barbecue ribs and drinking too much beer. Uncle Sammy could drink my pop under the table. Leastways, my mom told my aunt he could. Uncle Sammy was the black sheep in my father's family. Every family has one, and Adolf loved to say I was ours and make bleating sounds like a mad ewe until my pop would tell him to put a sock in it. I'd have liked him to put a rambler's sock in it, one of those thick tweed knee-length ones.

Old Man Taylor promised to visit the boy in prison around Christmas every year, which he did. He said that at least that boy cared enough about his mother to see her laid to rest.

I waved at Old Man Taylor as he glanced up at me and said, 'Howdy, J.J.,' in his resonant bass voice. He made Paul Robeson sound like Jiminy Cricket. I continued down the road, squinting slightly against the harsh orange glare as the sun sank slowly behind the cannery, making the pea-green building black as night in silhouette. I sang '(I Can't Get No) Satisfaction' as I walked. I slapped my thighs with both hands in rhythm to the song as I wandered along. I loved to sing and my mom often said I had a sweet voice. Adolf just as often said, 'Belt up, dumb-ass.'

I wished I had the nerve to smoke a cigarette in the street. I didn't, and couldn't if I had, as we had smoked the last one just before the world turned crazy. Or maybe I could show some swagger and call at Mae's for an espresso shot. Turn some heads. I had ten cents in singles to my name.

My feeling of wellbeing evaporated about quarter of a mile from home, when I discovered the sidewalk was coated in molasses. I was a wreck-diver in lead boots. My heart started to pound and my throat tightened like a noose inside my neck as I turned into the driveway. I tried to swallow but my throat was dry as a Utah tearoom. Beads of sweat popped out on my forehead. I took a deep breath and looked back towards the road.

I really didn't want to make it home.

– TWO –

I walked straight to the kitchen, bypassing the lounge. I knew I couldn't avoid them forever; I just needed time. I took a chocolate milkshake from the refrigerator and sauntered into the room trying to look calm.

'Hi, Mom, hi, Pop,' I said, as calmly as I could.

I screwed my face up in my usual greeting to Adolf when he said, 'Hi, brat.'

'Cecil, try to be pleasant to J.J. for one day, please?' My mother smiled a weary loving smile. 'How was Tony's mom, J.J.?' she said softly.

'Fine, Mom, she said to say hi to you.'

'That's nice. Have you had a good day? I hope you've been good.'

My mother worried herself sick over me, and I was oblivious to her concerns. Not intentionally; I just thought that she fussed over me.

'I always am, Mom,' I said, my voice trailing off. I lacked conviction in my own words sometimes. Adolf raised his eyebrows, shook his head in disbelief and sighed sadly. I felt like going over to him where he was sprawled on the couch and socking him in the teeth.

Sometimes I would catch my mother staring absently, smoking, wrapped in thoughts about who knew what. She was somewhere in her past, or maybe in a future she dreamed of, and I had no idea where. All I knew was that, wherever she went, it wasn't the here and now. There were times when I sat and watched her smoke a whole cigarette without even noticing I was present, exhaling smoke through her nose; and sometimes she hummed to herself, as though she were a little girl again, back in a childhood she rarely referred to. I could stand up and walk out without her knowing I'd been there at all. One time, as I listened to her humming a tune I'd heard her hum many times before, I memorised it, went up to El Greco's house and hummed it to his mom and asked her what it was. She told me it was from a musical called *Calamity Jane*, and the tune was called 'Secret Love'. She asked me why I wanted to know, but I didn't answer and went out to the back yard, troubled in my thoughts, worrying that my mother hankered after something other than my father and her children. The only real ally I had apart from El Greco and Bobby Stockton was my mother, who looked for the best in me at every turn. Though there was also my sister Lauren, who knew me better than anyone except El Greco, and figured me for a kid with spirit and balls. She was old. Eighteen. She was on some summer-school thing, teaching kids in Connecticut how to paddle a canoe, start fires and pitch a tent. I hoped she was teaching them how to put the fires out too. She would have looked out for me. She liked sex; I know because my folks had been worried as all hell about her going away 'unchaperoned' ever since she got caught kissing some guy at the drive-in movies. I heard them having a heated talk about it one day when I came home from school and she was saying that she shouldn't be treated like a child just because she had kissed a guy. She said kissing someone didn't mean you wanted to have sex with them. I think it did, though, because my pop said, 'We all know that one thing leads to another.'

I heard a lot of things that I wasn't supposed to. Some people would call that paying attention. Others would have called it snooping.

It was Sunday, and normally I would have been sinking under a turbulent sea of dread, but it was summer vacation and there was no school the next day. I should have been feeling mellow, but I jumped almost out of my skin when the TV evangelist screamed, 'Salvation! Brothers and sisters! Salvation!' from his cathode pulpit. I hated those phony-looking millionaire preachers with their bleached blond hair and suntans. All teeth and promises was what I saw. Jesus walked everywhere, except when he rode an ass (which always caused El Greco and me to giggle, hands across mouths, making quiet little quips like 'bust his ass' and 'quit being an ass' in Sunday School lessons), but these people rode in stretch Cadillacs driven by hard-looking men in neat grey suits – more like hitmen for the Mafia than emissaries of a church. They made me sick and I made no secret of it. I think they made my pop sick too, because he didn't send money when they asked for it, which they did after every sermon in every show. He would always say that a preacher's place was in a church, not on a television show. He still watched them, though. I could see no point in watching someone who promised salvation only if you sent ten dollars to the Church of Sacred Bleeding Jesus. It was religious blackmail. I knew plenty of people who were sucked in by TV religion.

Tony and I could buy a lot of cigarettes and coffee with ten dollars.

Missus Felton who ran the bookstore on Courthouse Avenue even took to selling second-hand books to make spare cash, to send to those gold-plated TV churches. My pop said some day

33

Missus Felton's second-hand books would put her first-hand books out of business, and then where would she be? She was driving away half her regular customers by preaching in her store. Mister Felton said she should keep her views to herself otherwise they'd end up retiring to Tijuana instead of Cape Cod. He said it once too often, so she showed her love of her fellow man by throwing a heavy glass Fire King rocket vase at him, putting him in Montmorency Hospital. She loved that vase. Forest green. With fins, like a space rocket. It cost fifty cents from a garage sale on a neighbour's front yard back in 1962. Anchor Hocking's finest heavy vase, in her opinion. Mister Felton received twelve stitches for his head wound and was discharged after overnight observation for concussion. He said plenty about phony TV preachers to everybody but Missus Felton after that. In fact he hardly spoke to her from that day, and sometimes when I looked through the bookstore window I would see him staring at her real cold when she wasn't looking his way. Mister Felton had murder on his mind.

I lay on my stomach on the hearth rug in front of the television so that everyone was to the rear of me and couldn't see my face. I felt better talking to people who couldn't see me directly. A bit like being on the telephone. I found it difficult to drink the milkshake lying face down, though, so I went to the kitchen to get a drinking straw. I resumed my position and sucked the chocolate liquid up through the tube. It tasted more like cocoa powder than chocolate. The TV evangelist made one last appeal to the gullible nation to make donations to help those in need (which I guess was him), and the show ended with lots of plump ladies singing and banging tambourines.

'Thank God for that,' were my pop's exasperated words when the credits came up. He shook his head and sighed sadly, just as

Adolf had earlier. Adolf got a lot of his mannerisms and views from my pop. Adolf was twelve going on forty.

The news followed the commercial break. Plastic-looking women going weak over juice extractors, grinning grey-haired men riding lawnmowers, and talking cats asking for more of their favourite food. The world news, followed by local reports. El Greco's grandfather said it was not the real world news, because it seemed only to extend as far as Los Angeles in the west, and New York to the east. He ought to know – he was from Greece.

There it was – the screen was filled with smoke, and sirens wailed in the background. Larry Judd, the KNTV reporter, who looked as phony to me as the suntanned preacher with his blond good looks and ice-cap teeth, started coughing as he began his report. His cough was as phony as his hairstyle, but it worked great on my mom. She said, 'Poor Larry,' and I just bet that little act got him in good with some cute blonde that night. He was the sort of guy women want to mother.

I gulped hard and sucked up the last of the milkshake. A horrendous rattling sound filled the room as air vied with liquid for space in the straw. I stared in dismay at the screen. I could feel my cheeks burning as I turned red. Panic and guilt. I felt sick, and at the same time fascinated by my ability to make the population of New Jersey pay attention.

I held my breath as Larry regained control of himself, gave a last small cough for effect, and started with his report. He really was a phony bastard. I couldn't hear the sound man or the cameraman coughing or wheezing. The fact that he was on the far side of the Community Lake, at least two hundred yards from the fire, didn't diminish his performance. I wanted to sock him in the teeth.

'*Six fire appliances from Cranford and Buller Counties fought house-high flames as a grass fire turned into a potentially disastrous fireball, threatening to burn down the Green Valleys Retirement Park here in Oceanside today. As I stand here, firefighters have now gained control over the blaze that, until moments ago, was racing towards the condominiums in this quiet development, causing panic and near hysteria among several of the elderly residents. Police officers and officials, helped by local volunteers, assisted in the evacuation of nearly one hundred souls to a nearby community centre, as fears for their safety rose. Over twenty acres of grassland and small trees in this recreational area have been destroyed, and police say it is too soon to calculate the full effect this devastating inferno has had on the local ecology.*

'*As yet, investigators are unsure of the cause of what can only be regarded as a local disaster, but police say arson cannot be ruled out.*'

For good measure he put his clenched fist to his mouth and coughed again, looking forlornly into the camera.

'*This is Larry Judd for KNTV at Green Valleys Retirement Park, Oceanside. First with the news.*'

I could feel Adolf's red-hot stare burning into the back of my aching head. He knew it was me. At the very least I was his number one suspect, and I felt a dose of his amateur sleuthing coming my way. I carefully flicked my head left and right to gauge my parents' mood. They were not paying any attention to me. I had to make a pre-emptive strike or Adolf would get in the first blow.

'Wow! Just look at that baby! Tony and I went down there to look at it and you should have seen it, Pop – flames ten miles high and smoke everywhere!'

36

'Oh, my, how dreadful. Those poor seniors at the retirement park must have been terrified,' was my mom's sole comment as she shook her head.

My father said, 'Uh-huh.' He wasn't really paying me any attention; he had gone back to reading his newspaper. I was relieved he wasn't looking at me in that glass-smooth accusing way he had about him when he knew I had done something but didn't know what. He was scanning the sports page when he suddenly looked up and said, 'It's a damned disgrace; it'll be those drug-crazed hippies lighting fires and wasting taxpayers' money again. The President should draft the lot and send them to Vietnam, make men of them.'

My pop had been in Korea. He hinted he had flown missions over Hungnam, but the closest he ever got to the North was Seoul, where he gave health education talks about the dangers of venereal disease to airmen who were more interested in getting drunk and sleeping with dollar whores than they ever were in dropping bombs.

He went back to his paper. What happened to the Yankees and the Mets was more interesting to my pop than the whole town on fire.

But Adolf's greatest interest in life, after football and baseball, was me.

I shifted uncomfortably when he leaned across from his place on the couch and tried to sniff my shirt. I started to move back out of reach but he grabbed the front of my shirt and twisted it hard in his fist so that it bit into my skin.

'Smell that, Pop – he stinks of smoke! I just knew it was you, John Joseph.' He always called me John Joseph when he wanted to sound old. He was such a prick.

Desperation swept over me as panic foamed up inside until El Greco's alibi ran smack bang into my mind.

'Of course I smell of smoke. I already said I was at the fire. Tony and I went down to the sports field to watch it; all the kids were there!'

'Cecil, leave him alone!' thundered my father. He was red with rage. For once he was on my side. He had already made up his mind that hippies were responsible for that fire, and nobody was going to associate his son with hippies. 'If I hear another word about it, there's going to be trouble!' He dropped his newspaper to the floor in finality.

But it wasn't the last word on the subject. Adolf pushed me back to the floor, reluctantly letting go of my T-shirt. I rubbed my chest, which hurt like hell having been nipped so hard.

'I know you started that fire, and I'll prove it. You and your no-good buddy will go to reform school for this one, J.J.,' he whispered, afraid our father would hear him. He looked at me real cold, so I averted my gaze. I hated him like nobody ever hated before.

Then my pop let me down so that I felt I could never forgive him.

'It *wasn't* anything to do with you, was it, J.J.?' He looked quizzically at me, his eyebrows raised and crushed. My mom snapped and said she was disgusted with the both of them. My pop backtracked in the face of my mother's defence of me, agreeing that even I had limits. The subject was dead.

I went up to my room, where I flopped on my back on the bed and watched my New York Yankees pennant flutter in the evening breeze by the open window. I heaved a huge sigh of relief and praised El Greco for his master defence. The guy was a genius. I took my BB gun out from under the bed and shot Elvis in the head.

I winked at The Doors and turned the radio on. It was over.

That Sunday had been one hell of a day.

– THREE –

Some folks regard childhood as their salad days – long, dreamy days of sunshine and green – but ours were caffeine days. We had decided the one thing we could do that grown-ups did was drink coffee. You didn't need proof of age to buy coffee. It was something that other kids didn't do, and we were willing to do just about anything to be different, to be weird, to be exclusive. We got the idea from watching *Casablanca*. Humphrey Bogart drinking coffee outside the Café Pierre in Paris with Ingrid Bergman, loudspeakers blaring, announcing the approach of Nazi troops.

It was a hit. We engineered invitations to other kids' homes so that when their mothers would say, 'What would you like to drink, boys?' and their kid said milk or soda, we'd grin at each other then look dead serious and say, 'Coffee, please. Black, no sugar.'

We never once said that without their moms saying, 'Sorry?' in disbelief and raising their eyebrows. We loved staying deadpan and repeating, 'Coffee, please. Black, no sugar.'

The only person who didn't look totally fazed by this act was Ricky Sullivan's mom, and she probably wouldn't have been flustered if she heard music coming from her panties and looked inside to see the Duke Ellington Orchestra playing 'Moonlight in Vermont'.

We even started singing lyrics like 'They've got an awful lot of coffee in Brazil' to make our folks twitchy. That worked too. They couldn't figure us out. It never occurred to them that it was a scheme designed to confuse.

It was brilliant. I guess all the kids' parents thought their ten-year-old offspring were little angels who thought of comic books and candy and Christmas. They didn't know the half of it. We thought about nudity and music and bars and motorcycles and what it would be like to be eighteen, living alone with no one about to tell us what time to go to bed or what to eat or think. We thought a lot about things they didn't even dream we knew.

The days came and went as the weeks rolled by. Periods of boredom, excitement and mischief all intertwined like vines and roses and honeysuckle growing up the gutters and trellises on an old house.

Perhaps the worst event of that year was my birthday. El Greco had turned eleven with no real fanfare; his old man was away 'on business' and we had barbecue and I gave him a Frisbee and a wind-up monkey that climbed a tree. It was pretty neat. Weeks in advance of mine I dropped hints like confetti at an Italian wedding about what I wanted. The big day came, so I got up real early, making as much noise as possible, clattering coffee cups and spoons so that everyone would get sick of it and come down to the kitchen to hand over their gifts.

It had the desired effect. My pop shouted, 'For Pete's sake keep the noise down, son,' a half-dozen times, until my mom told him he was making more noise than me and liable to wake the neigh-bourhood. So he came down in his dressing gown, slippers flopping. Bleary-eyed from snoring and being elbowed by my mom, who almost every day bemoaned a sleepless night on account of my father's snoring, rattling and choking. One time, in a rare moment of union, Cecil and I sang, 'Snore, rattle and poke,' to the tune of 'Shake, Rattle and Roll' at the breakfast table after my pop complained of pain in his ribs.

I hugged him around the waist, my soft face pressed against the coarse texture of his old blue robe. It was rough to my skin; a masculine sureness about it, and a scent that was almost indefinable, a kind of sour sweetness. We waited for my mother, who always liked to look as though she was in charge of herself in the mornings.

Adolf came down with a look of serious mischief on his face and said, 'Happy birthday, kid,' thrusting a small wrapped item into my hand. He pinched my nose playfully, and my pop told him to quit. He wasn't doing anything, but that was my pop's way of making sure he didn't.

Mom came down carrying a bunch of gift-wrapped presents with pretty bows. I searched for what I craved. Sure enough, there it was: a flat square object in gold paper that I just knew was the object of all those hints. *Big Hits (High Tide and Green Grass)*. The Rolling Stones. Our band.

Man, I couldn't wait. I was beside myself opening my other presents, quick as I could to get the process out of the way. I wanted to get to it and get it on my record player – nothing else mattered. My mom held on to it, saying it was fragile and I had to wait until last for it. She knew how to make a good thing worth waiting for. I opened the small package Adolf had given me. It was a temperance leaflet on the dangers of alcohol. He thought he was a real joker. I went to hit him with it until he pulled out another package from the pocket of his shorts. It was a pack of playing cards with famous baseball players on the back of each one. Joe DiMaggio was the Ace of Diamonds. I had seen the cards displayed

42

in Lucky's Sports Shop window. I felt a sudden overwhelming affection for my brother. It was not a feeling that filled me often.

I opened all the packages and for the life of me I can't recall what any of them were, except for a Day-Glo Frisbee, like the one I gave El Greco, which Lauren had sent me from Connecticut where she had gone to teach those other kids and practise being a nymphomaniac.

I just wanted that record. My mom handed it to me and, although I was eager to tear off the gold paper, I carefully undid it so as not to damage the record sleeve. The paper was probably left over from a roll my mother had used to wrap wedding gifts. She didn't like to see things go to waste. It was pretty paper and I liked it.

As I pulled the folds apart I could see writing on the rear of the cover. Thank God. It was a record and not a calendar, or something else I would have had no use for. I carefully took hold of the precious item as though it were made of fine china and slid it out from its paper shroud. I turned it over in triumph to look at the leering faces of the Rolling Stones on the cover.

The expression on my young face must have been beyond description. My parents beamed at me, their faces filled with love and happiness. My father said, 'We know it's not exactly what you asked for, J.J., but it's a real nice record, much better than that other awful racket.'

I stared again at the record sleeve just to make sure I wasn't hallucinating. I said nothing. Tears welled in my eyes and rolled down the cheeks of my face in stinging rivulets. I glared at the title on the record sleeve and read it again.

Country Fever. Rick Nelson.

I wanted to smash his grinning face with its pearly teeth and too

43

neat hair. I wanted to burn him at the stake. I wanted him to rot in hell. My guts heaved.

My mom put her arm around me. I loved them so much I couldn't say what I wanted to say, which was, 'Who the hell had this idea? Which one of you do I call Einstein?' I wiped my eyes and thanked them all for their presents.

My pop patted the top of my head and said softly, 'Why don't you put your record on, son? It's a real nice record.'

Breathing slowly and deeply, speaking quietly and trying to sound grateful, I said, 'I'll play it later, Pop. I think I'll just go round to Tony's and show him the cards Cecil got me.' I turned to my brother and said, 'Thanks a lot. These are great cards.'

I took my gifts up to my room. I was bitter and hurting, and then I remembered the kids from the orphanage, and what my mom had said about them having no one to love them or care for them.

Of the few things I had learned in life, I have to say that when a kid gets something wrong, it usually only affects the kid himself, but when old people get things wrong they really get it wrong. I mean, how many kids were sitting around the table at the White House making decisions on the Bay of Pigs? How many kids would have said it was worth the risk to invade Cuba? How many kids would have sent their older brothers to die fearful and alone in Vietnam? Eighteen- and nineteen-year-old kids not old enough to buy themselves a beer who should have been shooting baskets not machine guns.

I was just about to shout my goodbyes when I heard my mom in the kitchen. She was shouting at my pop. She said, 'Why did you have to get him that record? Why didn't you just get him what he wanted for once? The entire American way of life will not collapse just because our son gets a gift he wants on his eleventh birthday. Did you see his face? It's only a record, for God's sake.'

44

I left the house without saying a word. I didn't want to feel bad about wanting the record so much that it caused my folks to fight, but the other side of me was asking, why not? I had only dropped hints about a record. It wasn't as though I had asked for a motorcycle or drugs. I only wanted a couple of dollars' worth of vinyl. It didn't feel like such a bad thing to want. I loved the music. The chords hit a place somewhere in my head that triggered a sense of beauty in me so idyllic that I would bite my bottom lip and squeeze my eyes together and clench my fists, as though I was able to wring the very essence of my soul through my pores. I loved the music so much I wanted to bathe in it, to swim in the sound waves. I didn't want to bring down the government. I didn't want to fight the draft. I wanted to listen to the songs, to sing along. I wanted to hammer out minor chords and sevenths on an imaginary guitar. I wasn't a threat to anyone. I wasn't a threat at all.

I shuffled out of the gate and headed up the street with my head hung low, like a negro slave chained to others on my way to a waiting ship and uncertainty in a far-off land. I held the playing card pack in my hand, small beads of sweat forming between my skin and the plastic-coated case. I felt like throwing the cards into the air so that they would scatter in the breeze and tumble like showers of maple leaves in fall. I didn't. As usual the bubbling wildness in me stayed at ninety-nine degrees, never quite capable of boiling over.

A crazy desire to rip my clothes off and pee in the street came over me. I wanted to do it, just to shock everybody who knew me. Just so they would ask me why. 'Why did you do that, J.J.?'

I just wanted someone to ask me why, a few hours into being eleven years old, I was so mad at the world. If they had asked me

45

I would have told them. I just wanted fairness. Not a lot to ask. Just to be heard.

The moment passed and I didn't discard my clothing or urinate. I sometimes wondered how Martin Luther King Jr. must have felt when he was a kid. I felt like a bunch of cabbage in a pressure cooker. Something had to give and I knew it. I didn't know how to articulate it, but I knew it all the same. I was like my mother. I was a free spirit in a copper cage.

I saw Charlie O. out on his bike. It was a real smart street-racer. Electric blue. It had lots of gears and a saddle like a knife blade. It was beautiful. I hated it. I ducked into the driveway of the house owned by Mister Schwartz, the storekeeper, to avoid Charlie. I was too choked up to admire his bicycle and say pleasant things about it when I really wanted to smash it with a hammer.

I resented his bike because it was his birthday present. He was fourteen years old. He got a bike. I bet it cost a hundred bucks. Me, I got a record I never asked for or wanted. I hated surprises.

I waited behind the trunk of an old red oak in Mister Schwartz's front yard until Charlie rode by, and carried on up the road towards El Greco's house. The air was fresh. It was a beautiful morning and sunlight glinted off the alloy shroud around the base of the cannery chimneystack. A ragged flag billowed from a pole in Old Man Taylor's yard, stars and stripes rippling in the wind.

I felt suddenly ashamed of my selfishness when I looked at the flag and remembered the sight of that emblem draped over the coffin of Charlie O.'s brother Pete who had been killed in Vietnam, just in time for Christmas. The coffin was carried out of the Obranowicz house by an escort of marines while the neighbours stood around the driveway. My mom told me to stay home, but I went along to watch with El Greco. Curiosity killed the cat. It wasn't curiosity that killed Pete Obranowicz, though, it was an anti-personnel mine detonated by trip wire. The nineteen-year-old soldier didn't see the fine thread hidden by dense foliage for the heat and sweat running into his eyes. He had been making his way back to camp from a reconnaissance mission the day before he was due to complete his tour and fly home to spend Christmas with his family.

He wanted to arrive home a hero, with medals on his chest.

He came home in a box, his medals in a case on his coffin lid, on top of the flag, just about where his chest would have been.

My mom had stood by the driveway in the falling snow, tears of sorrow and anger mixing with snowflakes that washed down her face and on to her coat. My father put his arm around her to comfort her, and I knew she was thinking about me, and Cecil, praying that the war would be over before we would be old enough to be drafted, or foolish enough to volunteer.

I felt bad about avoiding Charlie. I realised then what I should have grasped earlier. The bicycle was Charlie's dad's way of trying to replace his blown-up brother, to take his mind off the boy they had both worshipped, whose life had been needlessly wasted. I hated the war. I was sick of hearing about the victories and of seeing plywood boxes with bodies inside arrive at Mister Jennings' funeral home. Mister Schwartz said the only people getting anything out of this war were Boeing from making more B-52s and the likes of Mister Jennings from burying wasted youth. Mister Schwartz was a smart guy, as well as a joker.

Guilt flowed through me and I followed my soul down a familiar path where I wished I could go back in time to wash my sins away. John the Baptist in the River Jordan. Excess baggage. I could never seem to cut the strings and let it all float away. Down the river and into the sea.

It struck me that if I ever did saw through the binding ropes, and let the sacks of debris float away in the tidal river, out and into the distant churning sea, some day I'd be lying sedated by sunshine and margaritas on some distant beach, only to be disturbed by the sloshing sound of water against fabric, and, squinting against the brightness, I would look down to see my old emotions by my feet. The thought sent a chill through me and I shook my head as though I could empty it of unpleasant thoughts as easily as tipping out wood shavings from a pencil sharpener.

I carried on down the street, my own weight lightened by the heavy load of Charlie Obranowicz and his broken family. I began to whistle the tune to 'Moon River', the words slipping through my thoughts like breeze through summer trees. I looked around self-consciously; it wasn't cool for an eleven-year-old to whistle old folks' tunes. My mom used to sing it when she was washing dishes or ironing clothes. She had a beautiful voice and she sang that song even more sweetly than Danny Williams or Nat Cole. I thought so, anyway; I loved to hear her sing. I could tell her mood from what she sang. Mostly she sang wistful tunes like this and 'I Left My Heart In San Francisco'. She was wistful most of the time, wishing she could start her life again in a land where she would live for herself, a free spirit in Paris, wearing a long grey herringbone coat and bright silk scarves, mixing with artists and writers and offbeat types. The confines of domesticity and motherhood were crushing her spirit like corn ground under a millstone. I sometimes wished she could open her cage door and fly away.

As I trudged up the incline past the old cannery I saw El Greco walking towards me. He walked kind of slow with a rolling gait, like a sailor who just got off a ship after weeks at sea. I gladdened at the sight of him. He had that effect on me. Everything was going to be just fine, El Greco would see to that. He grinned at me as I strolled towards him, and lifted his right hand to make a gun. His first and second fingers were the barrel and his thumb was the hammer. His thumb snapped down as he made gunshot sounds. Grimacing, I clutched my chest, falling against the chain-link fence that bordered the cannery. El Greco lifted the barrel to his lips and blew smoke back down it. I pushed my body off the fence and fired.

'Happy birthday, schmuck,' he said in his W.C. Fields voice.

'Thanks, bucko,' I said quietly. I was still hurting – not so bad, Charlie O had shamed me out of that, but I still hurt some – and El Greco sensed my flattened spirit.

'Let's hear it,' he said softly.

I told him. I felt bad about being childish, but that was what I was. I was eleven years old.

Tony understood. He always understood.

'Comes a time in everybody's life when they face a test,' he said in his wise old man tones. He paused. I waited, expectant as always, keen for his wisdom. We were now sitting on the steps of the loading bay of the cannery, looking out to sea and flanked by rusting cranes which reminded me of dinosaur skeletons; huge and forbidding structures of peeling yellow paint, splashed with burnt umber and oxide that ate away the bones of once-powerful beasts. We had gotten into the lifeless yard through a loose section in the perimeter fence which we had discovered way back and which remained our secret. We never took anyone other than Bobby Stockton there, and Bobby knew not to tell. One of the best things about Bobby – and there were plenty of good things about that chubby guy – was that he could keep a secret; plus he didn't smoke so we didn't have to share our cigarettes with him. He wouldn't have taken them anyway, knowing they were probably stolen.

'What sort of test?' I asked, unsure of where he was leading me, or what he was getting at.

'*The* test. Not just any test,' he said enigmatically.

I was confused, which was not unusual, as El Greco liked to talk in riddles, and wrap some things in mystery, like the best presents, hidden until the receiver chose to unwrap them.

'I've thought about this a lot.'

His voice was rich with activity. Undertones of grandeur rippled through his words. Whatever he was going to confide in me was very dear to him. He believed in it. Absolutely.

'Everyone on this planet faces something in life which for them is their test. Their big test.'

Whenever El Greco referred to the planet it meant that he was serious. There was nothing more huge or impossible for people to grasp than the concept of space and infinity – other than the concept of God, of course. But people just somehow accepted the existence of God. Infinity, though – now that was a tough one.

'So this is my test then? The record?"

El Greco smiled to himself as he looked out at the rusting red and white buoy that tilted slowly back and forth on the near-still sea. He turned to look at me, his smile fading slightly. His lips twitched hesitantly, as though he had looked into the future but couldn't see it clearly. Perhaps he had seen something. Something so terrible it had chilled him.

The moment passed and he beamed at me, showing teeth as white as summer waves.

'No, this ain't your test. That's what I'm trying to get at. The record is just part of life. Your folks were dumb to get that record. It sucks. The thing with grown-ups is they forget what it's like being a kid. They forget about fun. Everything is serious with them. They did what they thought was best. You and I both know it stinks, but they did what they thought was best for you.'

Then he added, whistling, 'But Jeez, for fucksakes! Ricky Nelson?' He shook his head in amazement and spat out into the water. He stood up and pulled me to my feet. I felt better. I looked out to sea and for a second I wondered what was on the far side of the ocean. El Greco was thinking the same thing too, or he was reading my mind. Nothing would have surprised me about him. I threw a stone across the concrete quayside into the ocean. It vanished into the great mass of swelling blue-green water. In winter the water was grey and forbidding, but summer sunlight gave this sea textures of colour so deep and bold it was hard to imagine anything more perfect.

'The Atlantic Ocean. The youngest and second-largest of the oceans. Only the Pacific Ocean is bigger.'

El Greco made statements as though he was reading from an encyclopaedia. He kept one by his bed and read some new fact every night before lights out. Knowledge was power.

'God, I'd give anything to see the Pacific,' he added wistfully.

He stood quite still for a while, gazing blankly at the horizon, his hand held like a visor to prevent him squinting against the sun. Staring out across the ocean to the eastern horizon, both of us fixed for that moment in time.

'Leads all the way to England,' he said, answering my unspoken question.

Then, turning west, he whispered, 'I'll see it some day, the mighty Pacific.'

His words were full of yearning. He wished it with all his soul. I don't think I ever heard such longing in his voice. It was just water and waves, but it was under his skin. He had a giant picture entitled *Big Sur California* on his bedroom wall. Sometimes he would lie on his bed for hours, just staring at the bright blue sea, its whitewashed waves crashing spray like champagne over yellow rocks, gulls floating high above a flat-topped pine.

It was a special ocean. It was his.

El Greco pulled two Kents out from his sock, lit both, then, handing one to me, dropped the flaming matchstick on to the water. It hissed sharply and bobbed gently away. We sat on the silent dock, legs dangling, blowing smoke, safe in the quiet morning.

'Come on, let's go to my place, I've got something for you,' he said, snapping back from Neverland.

We kicked a tin can up the street as we walked, the harsh sound of hollow tin against concrete, a crazy metallic cacophony. Old Man Taylor waved a huge slow hand and said, 'Howdy,' as we passed. We waved back and I shouted, 'Hi, Mister Taylor! Today's my birthday!'

'Happy birthday, J.J.'

His reply was loaded with sorrow. Maybe I had reminded him of his own two sons, or of Joan, who would never have another birthday. As we carried on up the road, still kicking the can, Old Man Taylor called out to me. I walked back towards him, curious as to what he wanted. He bent his massive form down towards me and patted my shoulder like a man who was about to shoot a blind old dog he hated to lose. He slipped something into my hand and said, 'Have a nice birthday, son.'

He straightened up his great mountain of a body and I swear a tear rolled down his mottled face as he turned his back to me and ambled slowly up the weed-punctured asphalt.

I looked at my half-open palm and saw a five-dollar bill.

'Gee! Thanks a lot, Mister Taylor!' I yelled excitedly.

He didn't turn but lifted his hand high in the air and carried on up his driveway and in through the kitchen door. I made myself a promise to send him a card at Christmas, and ran up the street to El Greco, who was sitting on a kerbstone chewing gum, blowing huge pink bubbles, letting them burst against his skin, then peeling the fine film off and poking it back inside his mouth.

'Wow! Look at that!' I said, holding up the banknote.

'Did Old Man Taylor give you that?' asked El Greco without a hint of envy.

'Sure did,' I said. 'Do you think I should give it back? I mean, what if he can't afford it? What if it's the last five bucks he's got?'

'If he needed the dough he wouldn't have given it to you. He's a neat old guy, though, that's for sure.'

That removed my concerns about Old Man Taylor's financial status, so we rolled on up the hill towards the Papadakis family home. El Greco responded as I broke into a sprint a hundred yards from home. We often raced. Sometimes we would arrange it, so that one of us would be the starter, with an imaginary flag or starting pistol; and other times one of us would simply make a dash for it. El Greco usually beat me, even when I had the drop on him. He let me win sometimes to keep it interesting. I knew when he was faking, but I never let on.

He was close behind. I tried to pick it up, but my legs were going as fast as they could. No matter how hard I tried, they couldn't move quicker. I expected to see El Greco dart past me, but he didn't. I crashed through an imaginary tape and raised my arms in salute to the cheering crowd.

He had let me win. It was my birthday.

I turned my head as I slowed, to see him lumbering up behind me.

He crossed the line and dipped his head down between his knees, his back heaving up and down as he fought to fill his lungs. He raised himself up and I could see he was sweating heavily, beads of perspiration arranged in rows like pearls, which touched and absorbed their neighbours until small streams ran down his face.

'What's wrong with you?' I asked breathlessly.

It was a sunny day and would be a hot one, but was too early to be making sweat.

'I'd better give up cigarettes, they're gummin' up my breathing,' he said, panting like a dog. Then he added, smiling, 'Don't develop those chocolate ones or I'll be hooked forever.'

I laughed out loud, feeling good now, as we walked around to the garden gate.

El Greco told me to wait in the yard while he went to get whatever it was he had for me. I sat on the rope swing that hung from an apple tree. El Greco's grandaddy had made the swing from an old kitchen tabletop, and rope he picked up off the highway. Dimitrios Papadakis was a scavenger, just like the seagulls that wheeled around the cannery before technology killed the plant.

I swung back and forth dreamily. The air was light with the fresh, clear scent of summer morning. The lawn was still heavy with dew where the trees cast dark shadows. The grass was growing tall and Tony's father would no doubt tell El Greco to cut it. That was one of his many jobs. I didn't have any jobs like that.

My pop cut our grass. But Tony's pop was a believer in hard work for young people. When I asked my father why Tony got tough jobs and I didn't he said he guessed that Mister Papadakis had to work hard when he was a kid so he figured what was fair for him was right for his kids too.

El Greco hated mowing lawns. He would push the mower about pretending it was Mister Papadakis and not the lawn he was mowing.

It took me by surprise when he thrust something in front of me. I had been daydreaming about school, thinking how good it was to be away from that godawful place. My grandfather told me one time that institutions are not to be feared, that it is people who cause fear in other people.

I pulled my head back to focus better on the object in front of me. It was obviously a record. I looked at El Greco.

'You don't have to do this.'

El Greco shrugged and said, 'No big deal, I'm getting a new one anyhow; this one has scratches. Hell, it's got ploughed fields on it.'

I could see that he had just wrapped it in an old paper bag from Sears. I didn't mind. It was the best present I ever had.

'You really don't have to do this, you know,' I mumbled, afraid he would take me at my word and take back the record.

'It's yours, kiddo.'

His words had finality ladled in them. I heaved a sigh.

He added, 'I bought you a baseball too, but I'm keeping that back for Christmas.'

I didn't mind; I was just blown away to receive that record. My birthday had turned out just fine.

I went home early from El Greco's house, which was unusual

because I usually stayed with him as long as I could. He wasn't feeling too good and Missus Papadakis said he had had too much sun. 'Too hot for a dog,' was how she put it. I carried my record home as if it were the Rosetta Stone. My folks had gone to visit my aunt and my uncle Sammy who had lost his job at the tyre plant, so I played it loud. The loudspeaker rattled so much I thought it would go up in smoke. I jumped around my room playing make-believe guitar, screaming out the words in time with Mick Jagger.

I loved it.

Uncle Sammy got fired for stealing. He lost his job after fitting four new tyres to his car and a fifth on the spare and driving out of the gates after being challenged by his supervisor, nearly running down the ninety-year-old security guard who tried to stop him. He really was the black sheep in our family. No one in our family had ever been to jail. Not even for speeding.

I felt a sudden blow to my ear and looked up in bewilderment to see Adolf glowering at me. He had punched me in the side of the head. He hadn't needed to, all he had to do was ask me to turn it down, but that was him all over: punch first and talk second. El Greco said that if civilisation had depended on his rate of progress we would still be eating berries off of trees, not sending men to the moon. He snatched the arm off the record, causing a tortured screech to rip from the speaker. That awful sound reminded me of the screams of a little kid running, naked and covered in napalm, on a news report from Vietnam. I hit him a second later. He called me a little bastard and said my record was puke. I wouldn't have taken that from the President even. Not being called a bastard, but him calling my record puke. He pulped me for hitting back. Tears mingled with mucus and blood from my nose, which spilled into

56

my mouth and oozed down my chin, hanging in strands as I covered my face with my hands and wept.

'Baby,' was all he said as he slammed the door shut. I prayed that the day would arrive when I would be able to punch the skin off him.

I cleaned myself up when I heard my mother and father come into the house. I didn't tell them about Cecil shredding me. I wouldn't give him the satisfaction of acknowledging his power over me. In any case if I had squealed on him he would have blamed me for starting it, and thumped me again the first chance he got. I wasn't the smartest guy in town, but I wasn't retarded either. I knew when I was beat.

I played that godawful record my folks had got me, just loud enough for them to hear it, to make them feel better. I lay on my bed with my fingers in my ears, humming loudly to myself to drown out the sound. God, I hated that twangy country shit. I went to sleep that night lying with my head by the record player. I had El Greco's record playing so quiet I could barely hear it, but it was beautiful all the same.

Tony was sick for days. Summer flu. Even his shithead old man didn't expect him to cut grass, or weed the borders, or wash his car. I used to shake inside when we were out shooting baskets or swinging from the tree and his old man would bellow like a blood-hound for Tony to come look at the weed he had missed, or to scrape out some tiny trace of mud from the white-walls on his father's car, which he had washed earlier. Little Tony Papadakis would tighten his face and look at me with swirling eyes, an edge of fear around them, and I'd walk round to the driveway carport with him, shaking, to view his pop's prized DeSoto, just because I knew his slit-mouthed father wouldn't whip off his belt and lay into that harmless child while there was a witness to blab. I tried to make it my business to be there on Saturday mornings, shooting baskets, when little Tony had to work his ass off. I had chanced to call earlier than expected one Saturday morning the previous year when Buddy Papadakis had grabbed his son by the shirt collar and smacked him so hard across his head that poor Tony couldn't see straight and blood ran from his nose, such was the force of that man's open hand. I think maybe Mister Papadakis was afraid I'd tell the sheriff what I had seen when he had turned, surprised, to see me standing mouth open, shocked and rooted to the ground. After that, I made it my business to be my friend's guardian as often as I could.

We both secretly knew that Buddy Papadakis wanted his car sparkling clean so that he could look like more of a big shot when he drove out to Newark or Jersey City or someplace where he thought his bright red DeSoto Adventurer with its superfins wouldn't be noticed by prying eyes while he acted the great seducer: seducing women whose only requirement for compliance was free beer and bourbon and the back seat of a DeSoto.

I knew what Mister Papadakis was about. I heard plenty keeping my ears open while my father chatted to shopkeepers and people from our church who could only whisper loud. El Greco never said much about his old man, but he knew why I came early on Saturdays.

El Greco stayed in bed and slept while his mom nursed him, and I got to sit with him some of the time and read him stuff from his encyclopaedia. I read him all kinds of things, like the height of Mount Everest. 29,029 feet. I scoffed, about that. I mean, how did anyone measure it? You couldn't exactly have a tape measure that long. Or maybe they flew a plane over it and dropped a ball of string down from it when they were level with the top. Who knows? I just scoffed even more. El Greco was sleeping so he didn't answer me about that.

He did, though, when I read to him about the Pacific Ocean. I told him that it meant 'peaceful sea', and that it covered thirty per cent of the Earth's surface. He just smiled weakly and said, 'I know.'

I started to tell him about the Mariana Trench, to the east of the Mariana Islands in the western Pacific Ocean, that it was the deepest known area of Earth's oceans, and before I could tell him how deep it was he said, 'Thirty-six thousand feet deep.'

Every morning I played El Greco's record the moment I awoke. I played one or two tracks before breakfast, guessing with the needle where a track started. I was pretty good at hitting the lead-in grooves, where thin crackly near-silence heralded something majestic and dynamic and beautiful. I had a routine involving the quickest wash – more of a splash, in truth – and one morning, as usual, I dried my face on the bathroom curtains. They were a pretty shade of coral pink. My mom made them herself. At first she didn't understand how the curtains became so dirty, then she got the deal. She knew it was me. It had my stamp on it.

Following my routine, after my daily impression of a person washing, I was sitting at the breakfast bar eating cornflakes with milk, maple syrup and clover honey (my own creation), when the telephone rang. I was too engrossed with the sweet mix of crunchy corn and milk and sugared honey to answer it. My mom came out from the lounge to the telephone table in the hallway, her form

59

fractured by the pebbled glass panes in the three-panel door. She answered it as she always had: 'Oceanside 4776.'

She didn't say much, after that, but she kept saying, 'Oh, dear.'

I didn't know who was calling but they weren't letting my mom get a word in. She replaced the receiver and walked towards the kitchen, her shape snapping in and out as the glass worked its eerie magic. The distortion of my mother disturbed me momentarily, then she opened the door and became herself. I sighed, relieved, and smiled at her. She smiled weakly and sat next to me at the big red-topped bench. She put her cool hand on the back of my free hand which was resting on my leg, my other hand still holding my breakfast spoon.

'I don't want you to worry, J.J.'

This was bad news. There was a tremble in her voice which nobody else would have noticed, but I knew. I always knew when she worried. I was like a dog that hears high-pitched noises inaudible to its master. Those words made my throat tighten so I could not swallow. My heart was banging in my chest. Memories of the fire came flooding back to me, images from hell bursting in my brain. It must have been the cops calling to say they wanted me down at the station house. How did they know after all this time? The fire was weeks ago. Somebody had turned me in. Nobody apart from El Greco and me knew it was us, so who could it be?

Adolf. His words rang in my ears: 'I know you started that fire, and I'll prove it.'

The snitch. Snitching bastard. I'd be going to reform school and all because of him. It wasn't as though we had meant to start a fire. It was an accident, for God's sake. It was just one of those things. It could have happened to anybody.

60

I resolved not to squeal on El Greco. No way. That was a point of honour. No way was I giving up El Greco. He was my best friend. We were blood brothers.

I looked fearfully into my mother's face and saw tears glistening like diamonds in her eyes. Her words hit me like frost, chilling my blood, freezing it to heavy black sludge.

'That was Tony's mom. He's in the hospital.'

Her speech fell into echoing whispers as she rambled on about some guy called Luke something-or-other. I guessed he was a doctor. I was numb. Panic trashed my sense of reason. I couldn't think straight. The fire and my own destiny were erased. I needed order like never before. My assumed cloak of maturity fell silently, and tears pumped into my eyes. I felt naked.

'Mom, Tony's going to be all right, isn't he? He's not going to die, is he?'

She took me in her arms and held me to her. I shook like a child. I was just eleven years old.

– FOUR –

It wasn't a doctor my mom had been talking about. It was a disease.

Leukaemia. I didn't know what it was, but I knew it was serious, because, every time an adult was told that El Greco had it, their brow would crease like corrugated cardboard, and they would suck air into their lungs and say things like 'Dear God' or 'Oh, sweet Jesus'.

My mom tried to explain it to me. She said that his blood was turning white, but that the doctors could turn it red again, and that we all had to have faith in God and pray. I had a vision of El Greco looking like Buster Keaton with his face all white. He loved those old silent movies, especially the Keystone Kops and Charlie Chaplin and Buster K. He would crack up laughing at Charlie Chaplin when he smiled at a pretty girl and acted bashful, shuffling his feet in those huge shoes at a million miles an hour. He would shuffle up Courthouse Avenue in the rain, past Missus Felton's bookstore, with his feet splayed out like the hands on a clock at ten to two, while he twirled an imaginary bowed cane in his right hand, just as though he were a miniature version of Charlie C. That was what we called them, Buster K. and Charlie C.

After my mother had told me about El Greco's disease I went to my room and played the record he had given me. I tried to fight back tears, but I was shaking uncontrollably. I bit my lip and folded my arms across my chest in a futile attempt to resist what nature had equipped me for. I held my breath and rocked gently back and forth but it did no good. My face felt ready to explode. Tears bit into my skin. I let out a low moan of anguish so mournful it was the loneliest sound I ever heard. It was as though it came from far away, so broken was its tone.

My father came into my room and sat on my bed, his arm around my shoulders. He told me not to be afraid, that God wouldn't let anything bad happen to El Greco, that God looked after little children. I blurted out in huge gulping sobs that God hadn't done too good a job for Pete Obranowicz. My pop said that Pete was a man fighting in a war, but I couldn't see the difference. They were both too young to die.

The words *good* and *God* flirted in and out of my mind. I wanted to say that the only thing *God* and *good* shared was three letters of the alphabet, that *O God* was just an anagram of *good*, but I didn't because I was afraid that there might really be a God, and that he would punish me for blaspheming by taking my blood brother away.

We got to be blood brothers when we crashed El Greco's bicycle, trying to make it fly like a rocket with us both on board. We had placed a plank of wood against a low wall in the cannery parking lot and raced down the slope towards it as fast as El Greco could pedal standing up, with me sitting on the seat of his bike. We hit the ramp like an express train; the plank dipped in the middle under our combined weight and suddenly we were airborne. We cheered and hollered like crazy men as we flew into the parking lot.

We hit the concrete hard, El Greco fighting to control the bicycle

63

as it veered dangerously on the dusty surface. The tyres lost their hold on the ground and we tumbled across the parking lot, two stunt men in a violent movie of our own making. We hobbled around the huge empty quiet square, both trying to outdo each other in heroic resilience.

The shock of the fall subsided and I realised I was not going to die. I had grazes to my knees and the heels of both hands: wounds that stung like hell but oozed dark rich blood, which made me proud of our endeavour. El Greco had come off better than me. I had on shorts but he had jeans and only had cuts to his hands.

It was my idea to become blood brothers. I had seen Randolph Scott become blood brother to an Indian warrior in a movie earlier that week. It was a great idea. We pressed our bleeding palms together and I chanted out some words that sounded akin to Cherokee. It was gibberish but it sounded realistic to us. We swore total lifelong bonds to one another, swelled our chests with pride, and pronounced our attempt at unpowered flight a great success.

I came back to earth with a bang. I was in my room and not in the cannery, the awful truth of El Greco's plight still unreal. I couldn't believe he was sick. It wasn't possible. He was Superman. He was invincible. I asked my pop if I could see him, but he just said, 'Maybe later, J.J.'

My mom came in and sat the other side of me. She told me to try not to worry, and she called me darling. She called me darling if she had bad news, or if she was really proud of me. She didn't call me darling too often, which was all right because I didn't do too much to make her proud of me.

I went into the bathroom and sat on the side of the bath for a while to think things through, to make sense out of it all, but, as hard as I tried, I couldn't find what I was looking for. I wiped my eyes on the curtain and went downstairs. My mother was sitting quietly with a cup of coffee, but her mind was obviously elsewhere. She was perfectly still, holding the cup in both hands. She made me think suddenly of a Vietnamese monk I had seen in a photograph in *Time* magazine. He was kneeling, dressed in orange robes, holding a shallow bowl of water filled with rose petals as a screaming Viet Cong officer pointed a gun at him. I recalled thinking how unreal the big automatic looked in the officer's hand; he was a tiny man. His face was contorted with hatred for the monk, whose serenity and belief were more than the officer would ever know. The report said that the officer had shot the monk, his blood spilling out from his brain as water flows from a hosepipe, forming a slow-moving crimson river on which the yellow rose petals floated, turning slowly like sampans and twin-masted junks on the Mekong Delta at sunset. I had asked my father what the Mekong Delta was, and he told me it was the point where the Mekong River arrived at the South China Sea, part of the South Pacific Ocean. I longed to see it, and I promised myself that when the war was over I would ask my pop to take me there. When I told El Greco about it he had done his usual thing and looked in his encyclopaedia. I sat fascinated as he read out an array of mind-bending facts. The Mekong River had its source in Tibet, wherever that was, and flowed for two and a half thousand miles through China, Laos, Cambodia and Vietnam, before it finally dissolved in the South China Sea. It was navigable for three hundred and forty miles. It was the tenth longest river in the world. El Greco had showed it to me in his atlas. He said it would be great to sail all the way from Tibet to the ocean in a canoe.

I sat on the couch and watched my mother. She was wistful

again, unaware of me watching her as she submerged herself in a hazy world of sunlight and unfulfilled ambition, or maybe some secret love. She was capable of so much more than she had realised for herself, and she knew it. In the way that a bear can be aware of the location of a bees' nest in a deep hole in a tree, so my mother knew of the honey of life. She knew it was hers for the asking, but taking hold of the golden urn involved freeing herself from the ties that bound her. One of those ties was me. She was a wonderful mother, better than any I knew.

She clicked back to reality and pushed her other world away, placing it back inside her secret drawer, together with the faded photographs of her youth, to be looked at another day. I wished I could travel with her to that secret place, to see what she saw there. I imagined it was a place by a river, where sunlight filtered through willow trees and played games with the water, sparkling like quartz on the gentle ripples created by happy fish who swam in formation in adoration of my mother.

She smiled wanly and placed her coffee cup on the table. She seemed surprised to see it in her hand, as though it had been accidentally transported from her private place, betraying her secret world to eyes that had no right to see.

'J.J., why don't you go out and play? It's a beautiful day,' she said, her words floating through the air in quiet melody. She added, 'Maybe we'll be able to visit Tony tomorrow if he's feeling better.'

I didn't feel like playing out. I was lost without El Greco. But I agreed, to keep my mom from worrying.

I left the house moving slowly, almost liquid, like the spirit-walkers the Indians believe stalk the plains. A person's feet mirror their heart. When I had a glad heart, filled with happiness, my feet bounced and floated across the sidewalk, gazelle's feet on human legs. That day my heart was tight with fear, tight and filled with concrete, and I had elephant's feet, my thoughts fixed on El Greco and the disease attacking his body.

I climbed through the panel in the cannery fence and walked down to the loading bay. I sat on a broken pallet and stared out to sea. The sun shone beautifully on the perfect blue water, as the rusting buoy bobbed gently, chasing the rolling swell. I took out a cigarette and matches from one of our hiding places, an old upturned steel drum we had placed over a brick to keep them off the floor and away from the rainwater that sometimes washed the dock. I paced restlessly as I smoked, my mind full of fractured thought. Only a few days earlier El Greco and I had sat on the same grey loading bay looking out to sea, when he had woven his magic around me, showing me that it was all right to feel anger at the world over a record; that that wasn't my test.

'*The* test.'

His words came back to me with intensity. Was this illness *his* test? Had he known then that he was ill? Was that why he had so carefully let me know that my disappointment over my birthday present had to be put behind me?

I felt sick to my stomach.

My insides churned and my heart tightened, steel bands squeezing it into a tiny pulsating pump, shooting hot red blood around my veins. I had never before felt so lonely. The value of our friendship burned into me. I realised that all the records in the world could never replace my friend. His smile flashed through my mind and I broke down, sobbing inconsolably. For once I didn't care who might see my tears; they didn't matter at all. El

Greco mattered. He counted for everything. He had done nothing to deserve this. He was a child, like me. I felt that, if he died, I would die too.

Suddenly scared by the thought of death, I prayed out loud to the God I didn't really believe in to save my friend. I made promises I believed I would keep. I even promised to like Cecil more. I resolved not to take my unauthorised cut from Sunday school donations; maybe that ritualised theft was in some way a factor in El Greco's affliction, and maybe I was closer to Uncle Sammy than I realised. We had, after all, shared in the spoils, dividing cigarettes and candy alike. I shuddered at the thought that God had punished him for my sins. Maybe I was to be punished too.

I shouted up at the sky. 'Do it to me, I deserve it, but leave Tony alone!'

Salty lines of tears ran down my face, which I brushed angrily away as my words drifted off on the breeze, heard only by the gulls that glided on thermals above the quay, their clamouring cries mocking me. J.J. Walsh, the hypocrite. I knew all about hypocrites, and scribes and Pharisees. It was what we learned in Sunday school.

I grabbed a handful of stones from the quayside and threw them at the gulls that normally delighted me with their insistent calls and symmetrical floating beauty. Stones hurtling up into the sky, and dust floating around me like smoke from a gun. I threw the stones as a form of bitter absolution. I guessed the birds knew I was hedging my bets, praying to a God who was less real to me than Robert Mitchum. They knew I thought God was just a name in a book, a word scattered like spice in sermons given by preachers I didn't believe. I started to think about Ricky Nelson and his stupid record, and how big a disappointment that had been to me, and how unfair life was. I wished I had been born into some rich family, where I could have all the records I wanted, and maybe even a guitar and a TV in my room, and a bicycle with more gears than Charlie's...

A chill came over me as a cloud crossed the azure sky, throwing hard shadows across the cannery. El Greco surfaced from the tranquil sea by the bobbing buoy, shouting, *Hey! Remember me?* Shame rushed through me, sparking in my fingertips. I ran as fast as my legs would take me across the dusty deck of the loading bay and into the weed-spotted parking lot, long since abandoned by the Fords of workers and Buicks of their bosses. I jumped the low wall and ran up the banked earth to the perimeter fence, catching my thigh on the jagged wire of the fence as I scrambled through. I didn't feel pain or cry out as blood spilled.

I raced along the sidewalk past Old Man Taylor's mausoleum, and into the front yard of my home like Jesse Owens, almost splintering the door as I crashed into the hallway. My father lurched out of his seat, dropping his newspaper.

'What the hell is going on?' he shouted, as I burst into the lounge.

'I want to see El Greco!' I yelled, fit to bust, breathing like a steam press.

'Who?' asked my father, perplexed.

'Tony!' I roared. 'Tony! I want to see him now.'

I was sobbing, my eyes stinging as I rubbed the backs of my fists against them. My hands were purple-white, gripped tight. I was shaking with rage. I was angry for forgetting him for a few brief seconds, but mainly I was angry with God for letting him get sick.

'Calm down, son, you can't see Tony now. I'm sorry. Maybe tomorrow.'

My father's anguish at my plight coated his words. He was powerless to ease my worries. My mother came in from the kitchen and tried to hold me in her arms. As she bent towards me, I backed away.

'I want to see Tony.'

Tears were pouring from me, as blood flowed down my thigh, staining the carpet as it fell from me in silent drops.

'You're hurt,' my mother said gently, kneeling down in front of me.

'I don't care, I want to see Tony,' I sobbed, shaking.

'Tomorrow maybe, J.J. Tony's not too well right now.' My father's tone was as soft as I had ever heard it, as soft as the day I heard him tell my mom about Pete Obranowicz, when she had bit her lip and wept until blood ran from her mouth.

'Okay, I'll go by myself,' I said firmly, 'I don't need your help.'

I was determined to see El Greco. I felt he would perish without me, that he would lose the will to live. I ran to the garage, grabbed my Schwinn bicycle, and hammered out of the driveway, changing up a gear as I went. I clanged the bell madly as I raced through the junction at Madison Street. Nothing came through, but I wouldn't have slowed if it had.

The Theodore Roosevelt Memorial Hospital in Cedar Hills was a way off. I didn't know which hospital El Greco was in. They could have taken him to Montmorency Hospital or off to some clinic in New York City or Philadelphia for all I knew, but something drove me on towards Cedar Hills. I had been there with jaundice when I was four years old, a century before.

I tore through the Madison Street junction and up Roundway Hill past Bobby Stockton's house like a kid possessed. I jumped as a motorcycle roared past: Jay Baglia, no helmet and hair blown back, riding his father's prized 1953 Indian Chief, one of the last ever motorcycles made by that great American company before they went bust that same year. Jay's folks must have been away because, every time they went somewhere, that boy was out on his pop's Indian. He had no licence or insurance, what with him still being fifteen and all, but he had gas and guts and that was all that seemed to matter to Jay. Mister Schwartz liked to say that that boy was destined for reform school, but neither the sheriff nor his deputy ever seemed to see him out there on it. Maybe they chose to let a free spirit be free.

I sweated hard as the heavy air clawed at me with unseen hands, my legs shining like teak in the dappled sunlight that fell in shafts through the overhanging trees.

I heard the faint noise of a car horn blaring, bringing to mind the sounds you hear waiting to enter the Holland Tunnel, to cross from crazy New York to half-crazed Hoboken. The tyres of my Schwinn fizzed on the asphalt as I hurtled up Roundway Hill and down again towards Van Nuys Avenue. I heard more honking horns and raised my right hand, middle finger outstretched, as I freewheeled towards Van Nuys. Whoever wanted to get past was an impatient dick, so I turned in the saddle to shout 'Blow it up your ass!' only to be confronted by the strained faces of my parents, staring at me through the fly-spattered windshield of our station wagon. I carried on down the hill, fearing they would bundle me into the car and take me home if I slowed to reason with them. I only stopped when I heard my mother shout that they would take me to the hospital.

My father picked up my bicycle and I climbed on to the bench seat where I sat silently between my mother and the door. Cooling air blew through the open window fanning my perspiring brow as we drove on to Cedar Hills, home to the Theodore Roosevelt Memorial Hospital. Everybody called it Cedar Hills, or Teddy's. My pop asked me how I knew Tony was there, and I told him that I just knew. He had nodded his head and remarked that God moved in mysterious ways. The fact that I had just guessed right was something my father would avoid if he could attribute greatness to the Almighty. I didn't mind. I was going to see El Greco and that was all that mattered.

We arrived at the hospital in no time at all, which made me glad they had caught me up. I jumped from the Olds as the front wheels nudged the kerbstone, causing the heavy car to rock. I raced across the dead black asphalt to the double doors marked 'Reception' in bold green letters on white. I pushed on inside and slapped my hands down on the reception desk in front of a thin-lipped sparrow of a woman with haunted eyes. She looked up sharply and was about to chastise me, but I beat her to it and said, 'I'm sorry, but I must see Tony Papadakis now; it's very important.'

She eyed me coldly and answered, 'I've no doubt it is, young man, but children aren't allowed in this hospital building unless accompanied by an adult of at least twenty-one years of age.'

She had read the manual. Hell, for all I knew she had written it, but I didn't care. I narrowed my eyes to maximise the effect of the threats I was working on. But I was spared the trouble by the arrival of my mother who, sensing confrontation, said, 'I am this boy's mother and we would like to see Tony Papadakis; he is my son's best friend.'

The receptionist hesitated momentarily, loath to lose an opportunity to exercise power, but she withered under my mother's burning glare. She flicked through the admissions book and said, 'Isolation unit, third floor, Eisenhower Clinic.'

Then she added triumphantly, 'There's no access to the isolation unit except for medical staff.'

Her words were confetti in a churchyard breeze swirling around in our wake as we headed to the stairs, hand in hand. As we walked quickly up the stairs I looked at the steps themselves, sand-coloured composite with tiny flecks of black and red bordered by a straight black line. Order within a building where disorder and human tragedy and relief and joy were all mixed up together; a peach Melba with wasps on top.

My father came panting up the stairs behind us, strain visible in his sweating face. I felt sudden pity for him, as though I were his father and he my son. I smiled tight-lipped at him, and he responded by patting my shoulder gently with his great soft hand. He came up the step beside me and held my free hand as we turned from the stairwell and followed an arrow's direction to the Eisenhower Clinic.

I was glad when he took my hand.

Being prepared for what you see in life is the gift of a fortunate few. Missus Papadakis was a crumpled heap in a battered vinyl armchair. Her capacity for chameleon-like change had turned Missus Papadakis into Missus Papadakis's grandmother. She was one hundred years old and I was shocked to see her. She looked up at me, black rings like bruising below her fearful eyes. She smiled weakly.

'It's real nice of you to come, J.J. Tony will be so pleased. You can't go into his room, honey, but you can wave to him through the glass. He's sleeping right now, though.'

She stood up slowly and put her hand on my shoulder, walking me to a window set in the wall across from her big red chair.

I did what adults did when they heard El Greco had leukaemia and sucked in my breath. He was lying in a metal-framed bed with crisp white sheets tucked beneath the mattress. Tubes sprouted from the back of his hand, snaking, like the air-line at Harman's Gas Station, up to a saline bottle suspended from a steel-poled hangman's gallows. Not long before, he had seemed golden-tanned, but he was pasty-looking now, like a jailhouse cook. 'White as a blind man's stick', as we described the New Yorkers who spent their time in air-conditioned apartments and chilled bars drinking ice-cold beer, escaping the heat and humidity of that city's unbearable summer days.

He sensed me there, I knew it. He couldn't hear me because I wasn't saying anything, but he moved slightly, then opened his eyes and looked at me.

He tried to smile at me but the love of life was gone from the face that could usually gladden my heart. His tortured grimace chilled my nerves to brittle strands of frozen heartbreak. I wanted to run, to escape the nightmare I found myself in, but El Greco needed me more than he ever had, and I owed it to him to smile. I smiled back, fighting tears, and his smile widened, so I grinned the size of a Georgia moon, and he smirked back at me, trying to outdo me as always.

I made our secret sign as a tear rolled down my cheek, and he did his best to return it without the use of his tube-filled hand. Missus Papadakis squeezed my shoulder gently, which I understood was my signal to leave, so I tapped at my left wrist indicating an imaginary watch, mimed that I would return the next day, and gave him the thumbs-up sign as I winked at him. He raised his thumb in silent confirmation, and I moved sideways as though I was on a conveyor belt, keeping my grinning face fixed on his until he slipped from view.

'He must have sensed you there, honey,' Missus Papadakis sighed. She kissed me gently on the forehead, and for once I wasn't embarrassed, as I didn't have even the slightest dirty thought about her.

'He knew it was me all right,' I said, quiet conviction coating my softly spoken words. 'That's how it is with us. We're blood brothers.'

I walked away down the corridor, head up, determined. I felt the world on my shoulders but if El Greco was going to recover I knew I had to be there for him. I had to grow up. I couldn't be a kid any more.

Silence stuffed the interior of the station wagon on the way home like cotton wadding in a shotgun cartridge. There was nothing to say. The trip home was instantaneous, a splash of water in the ocean of time. My thoughts were a whirlwind in the desert, painted dust swirling across a salt flat, stark against a blue-black sky. A kaleidoscope of tubes, of nurses in brilliant white, of machines with oscillating green screens and wooden boxes with brass handles, all jumbled up in a speed-freaked collage in my mind as the white-walled tyres measured the road from Cedar Hills to the old cannery. My mom and pop dropped me by the cannery without asking me why, and I got out of the car without telling them. I stood looking at the car's pitted chrome fender as it lurched quietly away towards my home, then, turning purposefully, I marched up the sloping grass verge past the cannery and straight up Old Man Taylor's drive.

– FIVE –

Old Man Taylor was sitting on the crumbling porch overlooking his back yard, rocking gently back and forth with lack of purpose. He didn't speak, just motioned with his giant hand to the peeling planks of wood once covered in flower baskets, where he had often sat looking at Joan. He didn't seem surprised by my arrival in his yard, where weeds broke up the patio.

Water poured through the sagging pitched roof in winter, but the day was salt-fish dry and the stoop provided welcome respite from the sharp sun. I was lost for words but Old Man Taylor didn't rush me, he just kept rocking like a flag in a July breeze. I finished searching for the right words and looked straight into Old Man Taylor's face.

'Tony has cancer, Mister Taylor.'

'I know J.J., I know.'

He paused momentarily and pursed his lips under his walrus moustache.

'It's going to be tough for him, and for you too, because you're his buddy, and that means you have to share his burden, to help him recover. That's a big deal for someone your age, but you've still got to do it because he needs you, and he needs your love. His pop probably won't be there when he needs him, so you have two roles to play, son.'

It struck me then how Mister Papadakis had not been at the hospital.

'His pop's business is in trouble, and, if he's going to meet the doctors' bills and all, he's going to have to get it back in shape, so he won't have much time to be at the hospital for Tony.'

Old Man Taylor was trying to protect us both from the truth about Tony's father, who blew his money on poker games, girls who should have stayed home, and whisky that should have stayed on the shelf. When Missus Papadakis mentioned Mister Papadakis's business, she mainly meant gambling and woman-ising, and Tony knew; he heard their fights, their hissing quiet-spat words at five in the morning when his father came home smelling of liquor and perfume. He never let on. Not to them nor to Katherine nor to me. But small-town people had a way of knowing everyone else's business. They didn't have much else to do.

I sat on the porch floor, leaning forward, supporting my chin on my hands, elbows resting on my knees. I didn't notice Old Man Taylor go inside, but he appeared back with two large glasses of lemonade and handed one to me. It was real cold, the way it should be. The glass was frosted with ice.

'I keep the glasses in the ice box, means the drink stays cold,' he said dreamily, and I knew then that he had gone into the kitchen so I wouldn't see the tears that had welled in his eyes as he thought of Joan, and of the cancer that had consumed her energy like flames on paper. I knew he had cried back there because his bloodshot eyes were misty still, their rims red.

'Mister Taylor, is Tony going to die?'

My voice seemed to echo around the porch, quivering like a saw struck by a hammer, nervousness rippling along the edge of my words. I watched his face as he struggled for what seemed like forever to find the answer for me. I trusted Old Man Taylor, which was why I had decided to get out of my folks' car instead of carrying on home.

He took a deep breath and exhaled slowly, looking down at the porch boards.

'I could tell you a heap of lies, J.J., or tell you a bunch of stuff I don't really believe in, but I'm not gonna do that. I used to believe in God, like most other folks I guess, but when Joan got sick I found my faith leaking away from me, just as the life leaked away from her. The sicker she got, the less faith I had, until the day she died and I had no belief at all. That's a sad thing for a man to have to admit to a young boy like you, J.J., but that's just the truth of what happened to me. Joan was a good woman and she never did a thing to hurt another soul. She wronged nobody, yet she was taken away from me and I can't forgive that. Her boys let her down after she was gone, but she was as good a mother as anybody ever had. It's tough to believe in a God who punishes the good and lets the bad run rollercoaster over the peaceful lives of ordinary people. My faith was like an elastic band – it just got stretched too far, until one cold day it broke.'

Tears welled in his eyes, but he didn't seem to notice, or he just didn't care.

'So I'm not going to tell you that Tony isn't going to die, J.J., but I will tell you that the more love you show him, the better his chances will be. He needs to see from you that life is worth living; you need to make some plans with him for what you're going to do together when he gets out of the hospital, so he has the will to get out of there. The doctors will do their part, and everyone will pray for him, but he needs someone to remind him of the fun that's past, and of the great adventures that are to come.'

Little pieces of torn lemon flesh floated in my drink, buffeted

78

slightly by an ice cube that I had rocked around in the glass. The ice cube was smaller than it had been when Old Man Taylor started to answer my question. As I watched it, listening to what he was saying, it grew smaller, its life leaking away from it, as Joan's life had from her and as El Greco's was too. When he stopped talking, I said, 'Mister Taylor, can I use your ice box?'

He didn't hesitate or look at me funny, or ask me any dumb questions, he just said, 'Sure you can, J.J.'

I stuck my hand in the glass, took out the melting ice block and carried it as quickly as my legs would carry me into the kitchen, where I wrapped it in a paper towel, opened the ice box, and placed it carefully at the back.

– SIX –

I visited El Greco every day, with no complaints from my folks. Either one of them would drive me to Teddy's, then sit patiently in the waiting area while I made signs to El Greco through the glass. The doctors were doing some weird stuff that made his hair fall out, so I gave him my favourite baseball cap and he lay in his bed with the Boston Red Sox perched on his head. The hat seemed to dwarf his face, which was starved of smiles, and thinner than the day he was born.

I prayed to a God in whom, in common with Old Man Taylor, I didn't really believe. I made signs with poster paint and pictures from magazines to inspire El Greco and fire him up over the great adventures Old Man Taylor said he needed to look forward to. I showed him pictures of baseball heroes, motorcycles, and beautiful photographs of the Grand Canyon, but mainly pictures of Big Sur and the Pacific Ocean. I wrote to the California Tourist Board, and they posted me great wads of brochures and maps and stuff, and I showed them all to him. He smiled wanly and stuck his thumb up at the mighty Pacific, and I swear I was almost able to hear its roar as waves the size of houses crashed into huge bleached rocks. I did everything I could to help him through. I persuaded the senior houseman to let me stick a photograph of Old Fisherman's Wharf and the basking seals at Monterey Harbour on his window so he had something to look at when I wasn't there.

Old Man Taylor was right. To this day I swear he was the wisest guy I ever knew. He was the only man I ever met who waited until you had said your piece before he weighed in with his own views.

He was right about Mister Papadakis too. Of course he had lied to protect our innocence, but he was on the ball where El Greco's father was concerned. Mister Papadakis only visited his son twice. Once was the day the ambulance was summoned by the doctor, the week after I won that fated race. The second time was when he came to tell El Greco he had to go away to work, that he had a big contract coming and he had to go to Seattle to pull it off. That lying son of a bitch was going away all right, but not to Washington State. He was headed for Las Vegas, with most of their savings, a quart of Jack and a showgirl who would have gone just anywhere with any guy who had a pocket full of dollars and a foolish streak.

Old Man Taylor was also right about faith and friendship. My pictures worked some magic and after a few weeks El Greco came home. He was skinny as a racing dog, but we were all glad to have him out of there. We had a party for him, with a cake and candles, just like it was his birthday, and I bought him a catapult so he could fire little stones at tin cans I placed along the rail of the stoop in their back yard. Katherine promised to place the fallen tins back on the rail for him, because he had to sit in a rocking chair. He still had to go to the hospital for special treatment and stuff but he was happy as a hog in shit to be home.

He wanted to know when his pappy was coming back from Seattle. Missus Papadakis lied and said his father would need to be in Seattle a little while yet, but that he sent his love to the boy.

The only person Buddy Papadakis ever sent his love to was the man he saw in the morning mirror, staring back at him through shaving soap and bloodshot eyes. Tony Papadakis never saw his daddy again.

Missus Papadakis struggled to pay the doctors' bills, but she made ends meet, and from some secretive little conversations I chanced upon between my pop, my mom and Mister Schwartz I had the impression that most of our neighbourhood had chipped in too. I guess it's every parent's nightmare, the prospect of losing a child. El Greco's grandaddy pitched his savings in; his shame at his son drove him to forsake his retirement and take a job at Harman's Gas Station, pumping gas in twelve-hour shifts. His troubled mind was only salved by his pride in the remainder of his family. His grandchild's courage was an inspiration to him, and to everyone who met El Greco in those days. He willed himself to heal. The doctors said they were dazed by his recovery, and by his guts. His fortitude was fuelled by his father's absence. He played the game with his mother, but he knew he'd never see that son of a bitch again.

El Greco kept a photograph of his parents in a little fake leather wallet he carried around in his pocket, trying to look grown-up. One night when he was nearly fully recovered he was allowed over to my house, so we walked slowly up to the cannery and sat on the loading bay, watching the full yellow moon shimmering, growing big then small in the inky swell. We shared a cigarette, a kind of celebration, something we had not done in what seemed like an awfully long time. El Greco only had a couple of draws but it seemed to make us one again, to mark the return of normality for us both. I sat watching El Greco through the smoke as it twisted, making it seem as though I was viewing him through frosted glass.

El Greco took the photograph out of his wallet and stared at it for what seemed like forever. He didn't say a word, but I could hear him breathing hard over the soft sound of the sea as it kissed the face of the deserted wharf.

I thought momentarily of shouting at him to stop as he tore the photograph in two, leaving his mother with half an arm where she had been holding hands with his father. He placed his mother carefully back inside the wallet and walked to the jetty's edge. I stood behind him as he tore his father into little pieces. He dropped the fragments over the edge and watched them as they floated slowly out of view. As the last piece drifted into the night, he let out a strangled sigh, a mournful, broken sound that hung in the night air. His words were dust on the soft breeze, and I barely heard him as he whispered, 'So long, you fucking son of a bitch.'

He turned to face me. I looked in his eyes for tears but there were none.

It was a long while before I heard him mention his father again.

– SEVEN –

El Greco and I watched the leaves change in surprising hues of red and yellow, colours we saw every fall, but which caught our breath and stole our wonder every year until the wind whisked them all away and frost coated the stark trees with a billion magic sticks. The snows drove stealthily down the highway through the skies from Saskatchewan and Manitoba across the Great Lakes and into New Jersey, as quiet as smugglers moving contraband by night.

We watched it all unfold, the jigsaw of life. El Greco grew, and everyone saw him through normal eyes again. I felt a rush of release when he gave me my baseball that Christmas. I held it until I had the feel of every imperfection in its near-perfect surface and the hard, raised ridges of red stitching mapped and imprinted on my mind. That ball represented something so wonderful that my gratitude in simply receiving it from Tony's hand overwhelmed me until salty tears rolled down my grinning face. That year rolled into 1969 and we all but forgot about leukaemia and worries and all. We listened to our records and spent our time with Bobby Stockton hatching plans to get rich quick so we could buy a Thunderbird or a couple of knucklehead Harleys. We planned to ride across America, tearing the heart out of life and shaming the winds as we went. My pop had hinted that he would take us all – Tony, Bobby and me – in his car for a road trip to Savannah where he had some business interests, so we planned that too. I didn't really hold out too much hope, as grown-ups often promised something but took it away again with some catch-all along the lines of 'that was then, but this is now', or 'times change' or some other bullshit excuse to erase their promises.

Tony and I tried smoking waxed paper drinking straws when we couldn't get cigarettes, crouched down behind the washroom cubicle door at school, and we found they weren't too bad. We were finally detected the day the school substituted plastic straws and we nearly choked to death on their acrid smoke, which clawed and burned our lungs, causing us to burst coughing and wheezing out of the bathroom straight into the school principal, Mister Barr. We got to stay back after school and write two hundred lines. 'Impetuosity is the imperfection of youth'. Mister Barr liked to confuse where education was more appropriate. I hated that old bastard.

Life rolled on seamlessly, or so it seemed to us. One January morning, great excitement rippled through the air as we walked down Courthouse Avenue on our way to school. We could taste it. There was electricity sparking all around us. We noticed a bobbing group of people outside Missus Felton's bookstore. Bobby Stockton was the first to run towards the store. El Greco grabbed my arm and tugged me forward as he started to run too. We gathered speed behind Bobby and almost caught him but he beat us to the open door.

He hit an invisible shield and froze. I froze too as I looked inside.

Mister Schwartz was doing his best to bar the door so folks couldn't walk in, but we were small enough to see between his outstretched arms and bowed knees. Missus Felton was lying on the floor with Mister Schwartz's jacket draped over her head, blood wet and shining in a pool which had seeped out from under the cloth. I couldn't see her face but I knew it was Missus Felton:

nobody else I knew in Oceanside had varicose veins that looked like relief maps of the Rockies. The sheriff's car came screeching to a halt with the siren going outside the bookstore, and the deputy bounded up the steps as though he was going to beat the final whistle and slam-dunk two points to steal the game.

He brushed Mister Schwartz to one side and knelt down beside Missus Felton. He pulled back the jacket as though he were taking the lid off a tin of explosive, and Missus Felton stared me straight in the eye.

She looked like a pizza on which somebody had dropped a fish eye for decoration. The deputy sucked in his breath and said, 'Jesus Christ.'

I always regretted not saying what occurred to me as hilarious at the time, and that was, 'No, you're mistaken, dummy, it's Missus Felton.' I would surely have become a legend in my own time if I'd said it. Ricky Sullivan reckoned I only thought of it later that day when I reconstructed the scene for some other kids at school, but El Greco knew better, just like I knew he would.

The deputy told Mister Schwartz to stand by the door and let no one by until the coroner and the sheriff arrived and to tell them not to touch anything until the homicide boys and crime scenes arrived, while he went to find the perpetrator.

He didn't have far to look. Mister Felton was sitting on the courthouse steps in his blood-spattered shirt smoking a cigarette. He was probably trying to save the system money by going direct to court. My pop always said Mister Felton was a decent guy, so that's probably what he was doing, trying to save the state some cash. He was early though because the court didn't get into session until ten o'clock, and that was only on Tuesdays. For speeders, mainly.

86

We ran down the street after the deputy and got to the court-house just as he was starting slowly up the steps with his hand on the holstered butt of his Colt. Mister Felton said, 'You don't need that, son, I won't be giving you any trouble.'

The deputy kept his hand on it all the same as he asked Mister Felton to turn around and put his hands behind his back. Mister Felton did what was asked of him and the deputy cuffed his wrists. He patted him down and had just started to read him his rights when Mister Felton said, 'How's your dad doing up in Long Beach, Lloyd?'

The deputy looked shamefaced and said, 'He's just fine, thanks, Mister Felton. Little arthritis is all.' He added, 'Is there anything you'd like to say, Mister Felton, before we go to booking?'

Mister Felton just looked lost for a second, then a tear ran from his eye and he said softly, 'Just that I wish I'd have done this thirty years ago, Lloyd; I'd probably be out by now.'

The deputy helped Mister Felton into his car, holding his head so he didn't bang himself, and they drove off smartly like a New York cab driver with his fare. No sirens, no fuss. Mister Felton had bludgeoned Missus Felton to death with the thick glass vase she had used to put him in the hospital; only he was better at it, and put her in the mortuary under a sheet.

My pop went to visit Mister Felton in jail while he was awaiting his trial, and he said Missus Felton just gave one sermon too many to a congregation of one. My pop said every good preacher should know when their flock had had enough. Mister Felton was seen by a psychiatrist, who said Elmore Felton was a decent human being who had just snapped like a rubber band when his overzealous wife pushed him one step further along the path of human misery than any man should have to take. Lots of people who knew Mister

Felton well, including his doctor, his bank manager, his minister and my pop, stood up to speak on his behalf at his trial. His lawyer said he had no plan to kill his wife, that it had just happened and that he was sorry for it. He said that in the ordinary way of things Mister Felton should just have walked out and not come back, but that was easy for a lawyer to say in a courtroom and a whole lot harder to do in reality, when the only life a man knew was built around the books he sold and loved.

The jury found him guilty of second-degree murder, so he didn't have to worry about the electric chair. The judge sent him to a pretty nice jail where he was put in charge of the library. My pop went to visit him with my mom, and they both said he was happier than he had been in a long time, getting three meals a day surrounded by his beloved books. My pop said Mister Felton told him he was allowed a big picture of Cape Cod on his cell wall. Everybody loves the sea. Even murderers.

The New York Times called it 'The Godspell Murder', and we liked to think we had some influence there. A reporter had come to Oceanside for the preliminary hearing. She had spoken to El Greco and me as we sat on the courthouse steps, right where Mister Felton had sat, and we'd told her all about what we had seen and what Mister Felton had said to Lloyd. We probably wouldn't have told a man what we had witnessed, but she was young and pretty and she had the sweetest smile I ever saw. She made me blush red when she said I was cute and that I reminded her of her old boyfriend who was out in Vietnam. She said she missed him, and I believed her. El Greco said, after she had gone, that she'd probably made that up just to get us to feel sorry for her so she could go back to New York City with a story for her editor.

We told her about the time Missus Felton hit him with the vase and about how she was driving the customers away with her constant quoting from the Bible.

El Greco told her that Missus Felton had let it be known that she would no longer be stocking the racier kind of books, and that Mister Felton had walked out the day she declared that *The Catcher in the Rye* was 'foul-mouthed trash', and ripped a copy right down the spine. She had torn the book after Mister Felton told her that J.D. Salinger was a genius and that if she got her head out of the Bible long enough to read some classic American literature she just might realise that, and then maybe she'd get around to selling a few new books so they could make it to Cape Cod for a hard-earned retirement. She'd thrown the ripped halves after him as he stomped off towards Mae's Diner looking for peace and calming coffee. We had stood on the sidewalk in the blazing sun sniggering to ourselves at the sound of Missus Felton's booming voice, but when she threw the broken book after him we sobered up from our intoxication and shuffled our feet in embarrassed silence. The book flew past Mister Felton and landed in the dusty road. He walked into the roadway, picked up the two halves and put them gently together. He ran his hand slowly over the fractured spine as though he had healing powers and expected to see it as good as new again, but rage and frustration had contorted his face as he stared at the dead book, which was broken beyond repair. We'd stood in breathless silence as he hissed to himself, 'If you ever do that again, I'll kill you.' He had turned slowly towards the bookstore, the book in his left hand and his right hand clenched in a quivering fist. He'd glared at Missus Felton's red and angry face and we'd thought he was going to step right up and punch her stupid bloated features, but he withered visibly under her burning gaze and turned quickly towards Mae's and sanctuary in a coffee cup.

We were the only witnesses, and when El Greco told the reporter the tale he pruned it like a rose, taking off the dead heads of Mister Felton's threat, and his seething anger.

We went down to Mister Schwartz's store the next day to read *The New York Times* and he didn't make his old jokes about El Greco being a proofreader for the media industry, or any of those things he liked to say, because he was just as glad as everyone else that El Greco was in remission from leukaemia. I wasn't sure what 'in remission' meant, at first. My parents had laughed when I told them that I was in remission from bad behaviour. I guess it cheered them up, as being in remission was clearly a sign for optimism for the future. My mother had explained to me that it meant that the signs were hopeful that Tony had beaten the disease, but that it would be some time before he was fully out of the trees, and we should keep our fingers crossed, pray, and touch wood. It was a kind of mixed metaphor but I understood what she meant.

The story about Mister Felton was there on half a page with a photograph of the bookstore and one of the courthouse with us sitting on the steps. She had sure fooled us. She had asked if she could take a photograph of us on the steps for her scrapbook and we had said yes. At least, I had said yes.

El Greco had said no but I'd persuaded him to stay where he was.

What we had said was quoted after a fashion as the words of 'two leading local citizens', and there were extensive ramblings attributed to us as direct quotes but which were obviously made up by Miss Beautiful Smile on the train back to New York City. We were relieved as all hell to find that we remained all through as variations on 'two leading Oceanside residents' and weren't named at all. The waves of panic that spread through me as El Greco read out the description of the *Catcher in the Rye* incident had me reminiscing about the day we set fire to the sports field, and my solemn wish to stay out of trouble for the rest of my days.

Mister Schwartz didn't object when El Greco wandered out into the street with the newspaper spread out before him, as big as a map of the world. He shouted back, 'Hey, Mister Schwartz, can we pay you for this later? It's got our photograph in it.'

Mister Schwartz just shouted, 'Have it on me boys, take one each.' He was resigned to the fact that he was a few cents poorer.

My father was furious when he read the story, not because our photograph was in the paper, which he clearly thought was neat, but he was mad as hell about the 'leading residents' who had made such outrageous claims about Mister Felton's relationship with his now deceased wife. He said if he ever found out who the anonymous pair were, he was sure he'd give them a piece of his mind, and that they could be sure it wasn't the pleasant part.

My mother said that the reporter probably invented the whole thing, so I played dumb and said reporters weren't allowed to make things up, that the freedom of the press was paramount in our constitution. My pop said I had a lot to learn in life, but I secretly thought that he did too. At least I knew who the mystery residents were.

I had escaped another scrape so I went up to my room and played records to celebrate. I played them as loud as hell until my pop shouted for me to turn the damned racket down. I raised a finger to the sky and flipped the volume up momentarily in a vague act of defiance before turning it down to his tolerance level. I knew when not to buck too hard.

– EIGHT –

Nothing ever seemed the same after Mister Felton killed his wife.

It was a pretty hard act to follow and nobody had the motivation to kill anyone after that. Husbands were nicer to their wives out of guilt for what another man had done. Wives were kinder to their husbands fearing that they would be seen as demanding and obsessive women like Barbara Felton. Either that or they were all afraid they would get a pizza face like that overzealous Bible-thumper. Leastwise, things rolled on calmly into the seasonal changes that marked the passage of time, and softly erased the scars of life, like the smoothing action of waves on cliffs.

1969 had fallen out of 1968 and brought good news and some bad, just like every other year. January 12th had seen the defeat of the Baltimore Colts at the hands of the New York Jets for the Super Bowl title. Sixteen points to seven in Miami. It had also seen the end of my New Year resolution to be good. I broke a kitchen window at Bobby Stockton's house with a snowball packed with ice that I threw at El Greco but which missed him by a mile. I decided New Year resolutions were just a load of old shit when Bobby's mom yelled at me and went straight out to see my father. The season of goodwill was definitely over. He grounded me for a week and took five dollars out of my allowance to pay for a new glass pane.

I spent the entire week wishing I lived in Florida, with a

well-meaning old aunt who was as rich as Elvis, and who let me do as I pleased. The problem was, I didn't have a rich old aunt and I lived in the wasteland of New Jersey.

The New York *Saturday Evening Post* had printed its last edition on February 8th. Mister Schwartz said it was the end of an era. He said that if Nixon didn't get us out of Vietnam the whole damned country would be gone to rat-shit. He said that to my pop when he thought I couldn't hear him, but I could.

The President must have heard him too, because he started talking big about the South Vietnamese army taking on the burden of the war, and July 8th saw a battalion of Ninth Infantry head out of Saigon's Tan Son Nhat airport for Fort Lewis, Washington; the first to leave for good who weren't in body bags. Those guys must have been relieved as all hell to get out of that war.

My head burst like a firework when I heard the cowbell beat to 'Honky Tonk Women', the greatest record ever made. I wandered around Oceanside in a trance singing that song. I felt so good. I felt as though I was someone for whom recognition was waiting somewhere – I just didn't know when, where, or in what form. It was a feeling that stayed with me most of my days, as though I was looking at a famous picture through sunglasses and although I could see it I couldn't quite make it out. It was almost at my fingertips, but I couldn't touch it. I could smell it, but I couldn't taste it.

El Greco preferred 'Jumpin' Jack Flash', the greatest song of '68, but 'Honky Tonk Women' stirred up a scene of smoky bars and big-breasted platinum blondes like Marilyn Monroe and Jayne Mansfield and the women we stared at in home shopping catalogues – so strong, it made me ashamed.

We sat open-mouthed, dumbstruck and electrified when the

Rolling Stones played the *Ed Sullivan Show*, firing music into us like X-rays. We couldn't see it, but something was laid deep into our souls like belief and hope in an ordinary kind of man. They played Robert Johnson's 'Love in Vain' and the words haunted my sleepless Sunday nights, when the ghosts and ghouls fought the dark night for possession of me, when my fear of school was eating me – voracious worms and snakes consuming in relentless silent orgy while the words floated in and out like waves.

I drove my folks to distraction playing those songs over and over again, until one day Adolf came charging into my room and slammed the lid down on my record player so hard that the needle skewed across the record, gouging the surface. I pushed him so hard he fell backwards. Another mistake. *Déjà vu*. I just kept on making them. Once again I had a bloody nose and a sense of seething futility when my father failed to do more than yell at him. I swore to borrow Mister Felton's vase and crack his head but I didn't really have the inclination for violence. Talking always seemed the best way out to me, but there was no talking to Cecil. He knew best.

I went to see Old Man Taylor pretty often, usually when I was troubled by things I couldn't understand. I had sent him a Christmas card just as I had promised myself I would, and I would talk to him about whatever was on my mind. He was wiser than a cartoon owl. He never seemed to sit in judgement of me, he just absorbed my words like blotting paper, and with the skill of someone who makes ships in bottles he would sort out my thoughts, so that I left there lighter in heart. It usually worked. On occasion we would sit on his stoop, staring at the moon, not saying a word, then I would get up and say, 'Goodnight, Mister Taylor' and he'd pat me gently on the arm and say, 'G'night, J.J.,' without taking his big sad eyes off the orange moon, because he was looking up to heaven, where he knew Joan was waiting for him.

One night, when I knew he was looking up at Joan in a moonless starry sky, I felt such overwhelming sorrow for his loneliness that I laid my hand on his massive shoulder as he rocked silently in his chair.

'She's waiting for you, Mister Taylor, but she's in no rush. She'll see you when you get there. You're needed down here a while yet. I need you and so does Tony. We all do.'

He smiled wryly at me and sighed heavily. 'Guess you're right, kid.'

I was relieved. I worried about Mister Taylor.

One day when I sat on the porch with him, I asked him if I could go inside his kitchen for a moment. He just smiled and said, 'It's still there, son.' I don't know how but he guessed I wanted to check the ice cube I had put there the first time I had gone to see him, a long time before. I just nodded my head. I knew he was telling me the truth. Old Man Taylor's smile told me all I needed to know. El Greco was going to be fine. I felt suddenly mellow in the realisation that we could now get on with the rest of our lives.

– NINE –

Bobby Stockton's pop died that fall. He had a heart attack walking to church one Sunday morning when the last red leaves were falling to the ground. Heart disease ran in Bobby's family, according to his mother. Bobby reckoned it was his mother's use of lard and sugar in their diet that killed him. He said his pop often complained that she cooked like her mother, and that her mother killed her father with a diet you could have run a racing car on. Bobby's father was thirty-four years old. He was five feet seven inches tall and he weighed two hundred and ten pounds. Bobby's father was a large pink bowling ball.

El Greco and I were allowed to go to the funeral. My mom and pop said I was too young for funerals but I told them Bobby needed us there to help him through. My mom took us to buy new coats. She knew Missus Papadakis couldn't afford a coat for Tony so she bought him one and said it was for Christmas but that he could have it early as there was little point waiting until December 25th when it was so darned cold right then. Tony's mom wouldn't take offence at that. My mother was a diplomat.

We got off school the day of the funeral. We thought that was neat.

I suddenly thought to myself that if enough people died – say, five a week – I'd never have to go to school again. But then I figured that everything else would grind to a halt, and people would be good for nothing all the time, so I decided it wasn't a good deal after all.

My mom said we looked as smart as generals and she took hold of our hands as we walked to church, my father lumbering along behind. Old people were difficult to understand. My mother obviously thought that a dead man would lie easier in his grave knowing that Tony Papadakis and J.J. Walsh had new coats. I just figured that what Mister Stockton didn't know couldn't hurt him. I was embarrassed to be seen holding hands with my mother, so I wormed my hand free of hers and ran a few paces ahead of her. El Greco joined me and we grimaced at each other, made our secret sign, and picked up two fallen twigs to have a sword fight. My mother took the sticks from us as we were approaching the church and told us to behave. It was a cold crisp frosty morning, with clear blue skies. The low, bright sun made it feel like Christmas, except for the absence of snow. El Greco said it was lucky Mister Stockton had not died later in the year, as sometimes the ground was too hard-frozen for the gravediggers to make a hole.

The church was a pretty wooden building with a tall, thin spire and a lonely bell perched up high. It was snow-white, and regal-looking against the red and yellow trees. El Greco once told me that the church was painted white so that the churchgoers couldn't see the bird shit on the roof, but I didn't buy that idea at all. I figured it was white because that was synonymous with God, and clouds, and heaven. El Greco said I would never make a town planner if I couldn't see the practicality in what he told me. I thought he was talking nuts. I had never once said anything about wanting to be a town planner.

Mister Stockton was there when we got to the church. Leastwise there was a short deep oak coffin resting on a trestle table in front of the altar. I couldn't swear that it was Mister Stockton, owing to the lid being closed. The coffin was nearly as deep and wide as it was long. It looked like a diamond-shaped packing case. Bobby was sitting in the front pew next to his mother. He turned around and looked back up the aisle to where we sat, so I gave him a thumbs-up sign, and grinned at him, to cheer him up.

He didn't grin back. His face folded in silent agony, his eyes crinkled like an accordion and tears ran from their corners, bitter tears that a child should never have to shed. I wanted to go to him but I didn't know how, then I flushed with anger at him for making me feel that way, for making me feel selfish for still having a pop of my own. I was glad when Bobby turned back towards the altar and his father's box. His mother put a gentle arm around his shoulders and wiped his eyes. She was crying too.

The preacher said it was heartwarming to see so many of Lester Stockton's friends at church to celebrate his life, a life which had been good and honest, and lived in a way which had earned him a place at God's right hand. It didn't seem to me that there was much celebrating going on. Half the people there were drying their red-rimmed eyes on neatly folded handkerchiefs, and absolutely nobody but the minister smiled at all. This wasn't my idea of celebrating. My idea of celebrating was fixed with the image of Mister Schwartz staggering down Courthouse Avenue and into Main Street holding a bottle of champagne, waving his wife's best black lace panties, the day the Jets beat the Baltimore Colts against all odds to win the Super Bowl in Miami, the day I broke Bobby's kitchen window. Mister Schwartz had kept falling in the snow but he had laughed like hell each time he fell, and never spilled a drop. I found out later from El Greco that the bottle was empty, and that was his third of the day. His wife had gone to stay with her mother in New York to avoid any personal embarrassment should the Jets be victorious.

It seemed to me that preachers were always blustering on about people who went to heaven sitting on God's right hand. Must have been a pretty big hand to have all those dead people on it. I thought to myself that if I went to heaven, which I didn't believe in anyhow, I would want to sit on God's left, as there would be a lot more room. I hated being squashed up in the back of a car or on a train seat, and that was only for an hour or two at most, so the prospect of eternity crammed like sardines in a can with loads of folks you didn't know or like seemed like a pretty dumb deal to me.

After the minister was done telling the congregation what a great guy Mister Stockton was, we all went down to the cemetery to 'say goodbye to a dear friend', as he put it. Seemed to me we were going down there to get even more choked up. I trawled down the short lane to the cemetery holding my mom's right hand and El Greco hung on to her left, neither one of us too proud at that moment. Soft sunlight fell through gold and magenta leaves, hanging still as chameleons from the grand old maples that lined the pathway through the cemetery, silent witnesses to so many dead men laid down. We stood by the graveside as Old Man Taylor and the other pallbearers wilted under the weight of the coffin, held aloft while the minister said a quiet prayer. They lowered Mister Stockton into the ground, and, as they did, El Greco moved forward to take a better look.

I didn't want to push in, but curiosity got the better of me, so I followed him. It was like that with him and me: we didn't like to miss what was going on. Bobby started to sob like a baby, and that started his mom off too. She held on to him, crushing his little round face into her soft chubby body. He wailed.

'I want my daddy, I want my daddy.'

That set my mom off crying, and half the crowd started too. I turned to El Greco with tears in my eyes, but he was passive as a wooden Indian. He looked over at Bobby and said, 'I'd give anything to put my daddy in that box, and get your daddy back out of there for you, Bobby, so you could have a real nice life together.'

Bobby couldn't hear El Greco because he was wearing his mother's body folds like hi-fi headphones, but I could see from his face that El Greco meant every word he said. It was the first time I had heard him mention his father since he had torn up that picture and cast him on the sea. It froze my heart to see the bitterness around his mouth.

I spent the longest time there. Misery hung in the air in textures as thick as frost on a park seat, hard breathing loud in the silence, broken by the nervous coughing of my father, and Bobby's strangled sobs stifled by his mother's breasts as she held him tight, afraid that he too would forsake her and slide away into the ground.

Missus Stockton, stooping, picked up a hand of soil and dust and dropped it clattering down on the varnished wood. She took a little more, handed it to Bobby, and he stepped forward and raised his hand, shaking up and out, as the umber earth fell into the hole that would soon be covered over, leaving only a piece of grass and a headstone to mark his father's life.

I was sore at myself for the way I had felt in the church, embarrassed to realise that there was no consoling a boy who has lost his daddy, and shamed by the fact that my pop was strong and healthy, breathing long and deep, wearing his repaired old shoes in his solid way. But all I could do was wish I were elsewhere – nowhere in particular, just somewhere else.

I looked at El Greco. He was off someplace, lost in regret or revenge, I had no idea which. The notion of revenge was something I didn't care to think about, didn't care for at all.

I worried that was what had driven Mister Felton to bludgeon his wife. Getting his own back on someone he believed had stolen his life, had scraped away at the seconds, which had rolled into years.

When I had asked him about it, my father said it was simpler than that with Mister Felton. It was just release, and the regret that he had not walked out for his newspaper one Sunday morning and not come back.

A sudden breeze rose up through the trees, rolling their branches in tiny waves, as though we had disturbed their tranquillity long enough. People began to drift away, one or two at first, then the trickle swelled, and the river of people flowed up the lane, and away from Lester Stockton, whose buried corpse embarrassed them now.

I don't know where it came from, but a force within pushed me across the space that had been wide as oceans, then I had my hand gently resting on Bobby's head, lolled to one side as it was against his mother's coat. I brushed his hair, its texture fine as beaten silk, and as I turned I looked to El Greco, feeling no great surprise to see salt tears falling in silence, the way icicles thaw in winter sun. El Greco spun on his heel, churning up the stiff dry leaves, and followed the others on up the hill, knowing as he did that he would never have the strange luxury of seeing his own father laid into the welcoming earth.

I stared down into the palm of my free hand, which glowed warm despite the cold clear day, and looked along my lifeline, as fortune-tellers do, and, as I stared, wondering where it might end, it expanded sideways across its margins, as did the little cracked lines all around it, until they opened wide and peeled away, and I was suddenly staring down a chasm of buildings. I was high up in New York City with streams of cars and buses below me, as chains of yellow cabs dotted along Fifth Avenue like Christmas lights honked their horns, and steam rose pale white from vents from the sewers and the subway. People in droves hurried along the sidewalks, collars up to the cold, and a bird, a seagull, blinding white, flew across the street below me, and suddenly I was back again in the cemetery, and the awfulness was upon me, as I felt the gloss of Bobby's hair against my palm.

Taking a handkerchief from my coat pocket, blue with small white dots, my father's, I wiped tears from Bobby's cheeks, wondering as I did so whether the harsh red lines of salt-burn would ever fade from his apricot skin.

Time, the healer. It was my grandmother's cure-all saying, and Lord knew that woman was a fading memory to me too.

Bowling ball Lester's own parents were both dead, spared the horror of that most unnatural of tragedies, the death of their child. Late-born to the middle aged couple, whose slow-paced days were suddenly full of diapers and strollers, buggies and knitted booties, Lester had been their Clark Kent, arrived as if by magic from another planet, conceived one Christmas Eve when his mother had one dry Martini too many beside the wide brick hearth, as logs crackled and spat, when the expectation of childbearing had long since passed her by.

Bobby did not seem to notice me dabbing at his face. In truth he didn't seem to notice me at all. He went on sobbing, staring down at the silent coffin as though the lid was about to pop off and his daddy leap out waving chubby arms, shouting, 'Only kidding, son!'

Only in the Bible did the dead get up. I could feel myself getting mad again at God, but I bit it down, because it never did me any good. Getting mad didn't do any good in any circumstance or problem that I ever knew. Strong will, or even stock-still patience, could get a problem solved, but getting mad didn't do one sweet thing. Mister Felton knew all about that.

There were only a few of us left now. Bobby and his mom, her mother, the minister, my folks; and El Greco, who was standing a way off up the rising path, hands deep in the pockets of his new coat. My mom was right: El Greco looked like General Grant in his grey coat with epaulettes on each shoulder.

El Greco's form was split by shadows that cut back and forth as the great maples swung high in the swelling breeze. The sight of him going light and dark brought to mind a flicker book I had when I was a kid of six or seven, where each drawing, page by page, was slightly more advanced in action than its predecessor, so that when you flipped through the pages fast it gave the illusion of a farmer milking a cow. I always thought it was pretty risqué, what with the farmer pulling up and down on the teats, and milk squirting into a pail.

We didn't discuss sex or anything like that in our house. I guess we were pretty conservative types in Oceanside. Over in Newark, or Asbury Park, they were nuts on sex, and out of state, in New York City, they practically did it in the street, any time of the day or night. Sometimes they hardly even knew the person they were doing it with. I knew all about that because Ricky Sullivan told me. He had family there, and he should know.

Bobby was still locked on to his mother, his little hand wrapped inside her puffy fist. Bobby's mother in turn hugged her own mother, so that the three of them in a line represented something so sad I could hardly bear to watch so I moved slowly on past my awkward parents, and along the path towards El Greco. My father had made a move to come to me but I just waved him away, saying I was okay, wiping hot tears as I spoke.

El Greco and I slid away, unable to face another uncomfortable moment. We strolled along Courthouse Avenue, hoping to get coffee at Mae's, but Mae was up at Bobby's house, making coffee and tea for the frozen mourners. Lester got buried the day Dave Thomas opened the first Wendy's Old-Fashioned Hamburger Restaurant in Columbus, Ohio. Dave was a New Jersey guy too. From Atlantic City. El Greco read about it in my pop's paper that morning. I bet Lester would be turning in his grave having missed that. Lester loved a good juicy burger.

We found ourselves out on the dock, the old cannery quieter than usual, the gulls out following a fishing boat a mile offshore. We shared a cigarette I had got from my father's car. I had only taken one, as the pack had contained just six, and I was smart enough to know when not to create suspicion.

At that moment I truly wished it did taste of chocolate or tutti-frutti, anything to divert my cluttered mind.

El Greco needed diversion too. He squinted down at his grand-father's old watch, which was kind of hard to view, scratched to hell as the glass was, and suddenly said, 'Hey, come on!' as he threw the butt into the water and marched purposefully away across the dock. I trotted to catch him up and asked where the fire

104

was. I hadn't used that expression in a long while, but that was ancient history now, and my fear of detection had faded far away.

'Where are we going?' I pleaded.

'You'll see soon enough!'

His words were a bustle of excitement, as though he had discovered something real important, more important even than dead Lester.

We carried on swiftly, out through the torn fence, past my house, across Laurel, and up Vine to the gates of Thomas Edison Park. We were crossing the park heading up towards Nantucket when El Greco stopped by the bandstand and looked across the lawns to the rose garden.

'Yep, got it.'

He wasn't talking to me, just thinking out loud. Then he turned to me and raised his finger to his lips to warn me to be quiet.

I followed him across the rose garden, past the cherub fountain, which was dry now, turned off at the approach of winter. El Greco looked up at a lone pine tree which stood tall from the thicket of elder and flowering dogwood that bordered the park.

'Yep, this is it!' he whispered, again raising his finger to his lips and snapping his head towards the trees for me to follow him. He took a quick look back, and, seeing no one, slid into the thicket, crouching low. I followed, heart racing. I knew it must be good, whatever it was he had brought me for, because he was loaded, his eyes shining and his movements suppressed, as though he had wanted to run to where we were.

We crept along through the thick shrubbery, keeping low, heads down by our knees until El Greco signalled me to stop. I looked up, barely able to breathe by virtue of being doubled over, and from fear and excitement too. The great spruce towered over us, blocking out the sun. I had no idea what our purpose was, but it sure beat watching folks blubber. I knew it would land us in hot water; it was one of those things that had trouble stamped across it. I was glad we left the matches back under our upturned drum; at least we couldn't be starting another blaze.

El Greco circled the tree, then told me to cup my hands and give him a leg up to a branch above. I did as I was told and boosted him up to the lowest limb, which he grabbed and yanked himself on to. He took off his trouser belt, looped it around the branch, fastened it in the first hole through the buckle, then let it dangle for me to grab. I jumped up, took hold of the loop, and pulled myself up, swinging my legs up to the branch. El Greco reached down and pulled my legs up by my pant cuffs, then I was up too. We were great tree-climbers. The hard part of climbing trees is getting up into the lower branches; the rest is easy. El Greco scouted around, and, hearing nothing and seeing no one, carried on climbing until he was as high as a house. He chose a branch and signalled to me to take my place. I clambered up, edged out on the swaying limb and carefully sat down. El Greco shuffled up behind me so we looked like cyclists on a tandem.

The tree faced on to Ricky Sullivan's neighbours' yard. I could see Ricky's basketball net, and a collection of barbecues; the Sullivans were big on barbecue. Ricky's old man was Barbecue King in Oceanside. His chilli ribs were voted best. They were good, too. Better even than Denny's.

'What's goin' on? Why the fuck are we up here?' I asked El Greco, whispering, partly out of fear of being overheard by whoever might have been around, but mainly worried that too much exertion might cause me to lose my precarious perch.

'You'll see. Just be quiet and fucking keep still.'

I still had no clue what it was that took so much trouble but I hoped it was worth it.

Moments later El Greco gripped my arm. 'Showtime!' he hissed excitedly.

Ricky's neighbours let out their house, usually to smart young business people who dressed in Brooks Brothers suits and wore horn-rimmed spectacles. Geeky types. The Cook family home had long glass windows along the top floor, with a balcony terrace where on summer evenings they sat above Thomas Edison Park, drinking vodka Martinis and smoking, looking out through the gaps in the trees over the neat lawns and tennis courts to the ocean.

The current renters were artists who were supposed to be famous, but they couldn't have been up to much because I had never heard of them.

El Greco let go of my arm and whispered, 'Don't move about: watch that window!'

I stared straight ahead, afraid to miss a thing. I felt a bit weird, like a bird up in the tree, and a strange bird at that, what with all the staring I was doing. The couple had appeared in the room and El Greco whispered in my ear, 'Good old Ricky, and I didn't believe him either. Bang on time too.'

They were stark naked! I couldn't believe my eyes. Naked as could be, except for the man's spectacles, which were round and hippy-looking. He looked funny as hell, what with his thingy and his goofy glasses. She was great to look at. I'd never seen a real naked woman before, except in a book El Greco's crummy old man hid under his car seat. Another marvellous find when we were looking for cigarettes, but somehow we didn't want to look at it much, as I guessed that Mister Papadakis was probably looking at real naked women when he was 'away on business' and that made everything dirty and put the liar's mark firmly over him. I'd seen El Greco's mom's bare boobies, of course, but this woman was as naked as could be. Not a stitch on.

There was music coming from the house, real loud hippy music, the type my pop hated. The Velvet something. They had a woman singer who sounded like a man. When that kind of stuff came on the radio he just turned it off, or tuned it to the country station.

There was a big canvas on an easel with some squiggly lines and rainbow-type stuff on it. Jeez, I could have done a better picture than that. No wonder I hadn't heard of them. Their stuff looked like a kid did it.

Old Speccy Eyes got a big brush and started dancing around the girl, splashing bits of bright red paint on her milk-white body. His thing was bouncing around like a twirly wooden clacker, the type people whirled at football games. It was hysterical. El Greco started shaking with laughter, holding it in, then so did I. I tried to stop but it overtook me and tears ran down my cheeks. I was laughing fit to bust my guts. I'd have given anything to be on that balcony, having a real close look. I could barely see through my tears. Laughing out loud now, overtaken by the ridiculousness of it all.

Then I was falling like a stone, branches buffeting my body and twigs and leathery fronds thwacking my face. My coat caught on an old broken branch, but before I had time to register my good fortune the momentum of my fall swung me around into the tree trunk with a sharp cracking sound. At first I thought the branch was breaking under my weight, but the sudden pain made me realise the sound was me.

108

So there I was, hanging like a squirrel, facing the ground twenty feet below, with my collarbone snapped like a twig.

El Greco was calling to me, panic in his voice. 'J.J., are you all right? Are you all right, J.J.?'

I couldn't answer, pain being what it is. He called to me again, then I heard him scrambling down the tree.

'Wow! That was lucky!' he boomed. 'I thought you'd gone all the way!'

'I'm hurt,' I said, teeth gritted.

'Bad?' Quiet now. Scared. I couldn't see him, but I could hear it in his voice. His voice cracked like it did when Buddy Papadakis would call his name with an edge of anger to it, and he would shout back, 'Coming, Daddy' and slope off to meet his fate, followed by me with my racing heart, his frightened guardian. El Greco didn't frighten easily.

'Get help!' I gasped.

'I will! Don't move! I'll be right back!'

He shinned down the tree and I heard bushes rustling as he rushed away. *Don't move*? I could hardly breathe for pain, so I wasn't about to move. For once I was perfectly still, terrified that the old branch would give way and send me spinning to the ground below.

After what seemed like forever, I heard the distant wail of sirens, the sounds of movement below me, of branches being brushed, and then a shimmery voice saying, 'Hey there, how you doin'?'

I opened my clenched eyes and stared down, misty-eyed. I was clearly hallucinating from the pain, and the shock of the bone break: I imagined that a television camera was pointing up at me. I shut my eyes and opened them again. I was still hallucinating. It still looked like a television camera, and behind it was the back side of a baseball cap with the letters KNTV showing, and the pearly white teeth of a black man, so I knew I was dreaming, as I never saw a negro in Oceanside except for Forest Johnson, and he wasn't no cameraman. He sold insurance up in Newark to folks who could just about afford his company's bottom-end life policies. They bought the policies to pay for their own funerals. My father told me that. He told me it was 'ironic', whatever that meant. Missus Felton had said it was 'the beginning of the end' when Forest and his wife and kids moved down from Newark after the nightmare events of '67 when twenty-six people had died in six days of bloody riots there, and the National Guard had gone berserk. Leastways, that was what I heard Mister Schwartz say to Missus Felton while I was buying gum, about the National Guard going bananas and all, and I swear I heard Missus Felton say back, 'Those niggers got what they deserved.' I had never heard anyone except folks on TV news refer to negroes as niggers.

One time she had said that thing to my mother about the Johnsons moving to Oceanside from Newark being 'the beginning of the end' while we were in her store buying school readers. My mom said, 'Oh, I don't know, might be good to have some new folks around this place.' Mister Felton made a comment about Missus Felton being bigoted, whatever that meant, and Missus Felton just turned bright red and snapped, 'Are you forgetting what those people did up in Newark? Do you want uppity types moving in here and bringing their troubles down on their betters? I'm sure none of us wants that, do we, Bryony?'

My mother didn't answer, just ushered me out of the store. She took my hand and told me that I was never to listen to anything Missus Felton had to say on the subject of coloureds. Some Christian Missus Felton was.

I told my mom what Tony told me: that his old man had told Katherine to stay away from the Johnson kids who were in her school class, and to never bring them to their house. Tony's mom had said they could bring whoever they wished home after school, but Buddy had slammed his hand down on the dinner table and said, 'Those people will never set foot under this roof.' They were twin girls. I didn't see the problem. We didn't play with them because they were too young and they were girls. If they'd been older, and boys, we'd have played with them. Hell, we'd probably have let them share our cigarettes.

My mother said the Lord created us all equal, and that meant all people, not just white people. She seemed pretty mad at Missus Felton, and I guess at Buddy Papadakis too. I asked my pop about it later and he said there were people in this town who hated other people for no good reason, negroes in particular, and that I was to treat people as I found them to be, and not judge them by the colour of their skin, or the way they spoke. He said there was an unpleasant side to more people than I imagined in our little town, and that ignorant and hateful people so often produced ignorant and hateful sons, and that the older I got, the more I'd realise that.

Tony's pop was one of those hateful types, but Tony wasn't, so I figured Pop was talking shit. He seemed pretty cross about it, though. He patted my head as if to show me that we were on the good side. What about people from the South? I asked him. They all talk funny, black or white. My father had laughed at that.

I blinked my eyes open again, and thought I saw an angel looking up at me, golden hair shining. Then I heard the voice again, and I knew I was dreaming. It sounded like Larry Judd, and I could have sworn I heard him say, 'KNTV. First with the news.'

Then I heard more voices and someone saying, 'Get the hell out

111

of here,' and then El Greco shouting, 'It's okay, J.J. The ambulance is here!'

Sure enough, there was an ambulance. Two police cars. A fire truck. A woman with a dog. And a television crew. Just my luck.

That evening I had the dubious pleasure of lying in a hospital bed, surrounded by El Greco, my parents, Adolf, Katherine, Missus Papadakis, Lauren who was home from college, two doctors, and a quartet of giggly nurses, as Larry Judd beamed out from the screen. The shot kept cutting back and forth from Larry to me, hanging in my new coat, face grazed and bloody, for all the world like a wombat in mid-flight.

I'd have been embarrassed as all hell if I hadn't been feeling so banged about.

They showed El Greco staring up, a paramedic climbing the tree, the firemen placing their ladder against it, and then them winching me down in a cradle, like a big baby in a giant diaper. Christ, the whole town must be laughing at me. I'd never be able to live in New Jersey again. They'd be watching me in Trenton. And probably Asbury Park and Camden too.

'Tragedy struck one of Oceanside's younger residents today when a bird-egg-collecting mission in Thomas Edison Park went badly wrong. Along with his schoolmate Tony Papadakis, eleven-year-old John Joseph Walsh, or J.J. as he is known in these parts, climbed this tree in search of kestrel eggs, having seen what the pair believed to be a kestrel in the upper branches. Sadly for J.J., when he was almost within reach of the nest he lost his footing and fell almost twenty feet, when by extraordinary luck his fall was arrested by a broken tree limb that inserted itself inside his overcoat. Having suffered what paramedics state is a fractured

collarbone he was unable to extricate himself, so the plucky guy waited for help to arrive. He was rescued by Cranford County firefighters and rushed to Theodore Roosevelt Memorial Hospital, Cedar Hills, where he will be treated for fractures, cuts and bruises. This is Larry Judd in Thomas Edison Park, Oceanside, for KNTV. First with the news.'

El Greco was brilliant. Only he could come up with a story like that. Completely believable, and no one any the wiser. Except for Adolf, who said, 'Oh, yeah, right,' when I related the tale to my worried parents at the hospital.

Larry and his cameraman had been heading for Trenton and on the north side of Thomas Edison Park when they heard the call on their radio, tuned to the police band. Just my luck that they got to El Greco before anyone else. El Greco said that Golden-Hair-Larry had his life history down in under ten seconds and he was off running, leaving little Tony Papadakis to wait for the cops and the ambulance.

Still, we got to be famous. We got to be on television, although I didn't look my best.

Ricky Sullivan came to visit me the next morning. He was all excited. His aunt from New York had called his mother to tell her she had seen their house on the nine o'clock news. We even made it to New York! Ricky guessed what we had been about, but he kept it to himself. He had only told El Greco and afterwards wished he hadn't. He said that sometimes he played sick to get off school so he could hide in his pop's toolshed and watch them prancing and painting naked, but he was certain you could go to prison for peeping at naked people, so he kept quiet about it.

Breaking a collarbone is no pleasant thing. The surgeon told me all about it, about the clavicle being a floating type of bone and how it was attached to your ribs and shoulder with ligaments and stuff. He said I'd heal just fine because I was young and healthy, and that I just needed to take things easy for a while, and not climb any more trees. He said birds' eggs are better left to become birds. I told him I guessed they were. I had no intention of ever climbing another tree.

– TEN –

1970. Another year gone by with astounding and unremarkable things marking the forward roll of time. We missed out on a claim to fame when just about every paper in the country printed a photograph of some woman's belly with splashes of paint surrounding one of those circles with the upside-down letter Y and stuff in it. It was a protest thing called 'Artists Against The War'. We could have told anyone who cared to listen that the paint in the black and white photograph was pink and red: we'd seen it in the flesh. The paint represented flesh and blood. My pop had held it up to show my mother, who wasn't the least bit interested in his views, as she knew he'd say something like, 'What the heck has that got to do with art?'

He actually said, 'Why on earth do they print this stuff?'

My mom gave him a brief smile and said, 'Perhaps they have a point, dear.'

To which my pop replied, 'I'd give them the point. The point of my shoe.'

Midsummer found El Greco and me sitting in the Roadway Diner drinking coffee with Bobby. We were still drinking it black, no sugar. We weren't trying to shock folks any more, it had just become a thing we did.

We were listening to the jukebox, immersed in checking out

places and things of interest we might see on a drive we were to take with my father to Georgia – as he put it, 'to give all our poor mothers some well-deserved peace', as though we were all trouble and pains in the ass. I had pretty much given up on his veiled promise to take Tony, Bobby and me to Savannah, but my old man was full of surprises. Thankfully he had had the good sense to tell Adolf he needed to stay home as man of the house while he was gone. That would have been some trip: El Greco and Bobby and me and Adolf. I'd rather have been dragged naked by my dick through Oceanside on Thanksgiving. Cecil's every move around me was still laden with suspicion, mistrust and derision. Some guy.

We often whiled away hours with a copy of *New Horizons World Guide*, Pan American Airways' guide to everything worth a light. It was the best book ever. Dimitrios Papadakis had given it to Tony while he was recovering, hoping to fire up his grandson's hope and enthusiasm, and ever since we had spent hours glued to that book – as much our Bible as the New Testament ever was for my father. Page 165 gave a general overview of Georgia, and its industries, geography, and major points of interest like Vogel State Park, and Chattahoochee National Forest, but pages 208 to 211 explained a whole bunch of stuff about Savannah, so that we longed even harder for the day we would leave on our long-promised trip. Stepping into the unknown. I never remarked on the first entry under 'Accommodations' that listed the DeSoto Hotel. Single from $4, double from $9. I figured the name of Buddy Papadakis's car linked to a hotel was not lost on El Greco, who, while Katherine slept quiet and oblivious, had heard many a heated late-night spat between his parents over hotel bills left in suit pockets or the glove-box in his car, for which he could give no good account save to get threatening towards Tony's mom, who would then let it drop for the sake of her children, Buddy's little victory signalled by Missus Papadakis throwing a blanket and pillow down the stairwell before closing their bedroom door to reinforce the fact that Buddy would be spending that night on the couch. These were the things that made that pretty woman ninety years old.

We dreamed big in our make-believe plans for our trip to Savannah, and for our great ambition, our journey to the ocean. Not the Atlantic Ocean, which was at our door, but the mighty Pacific, over two thousand miles away. The stuff of Tony Papadakis's dreams. We were filled with curiosity, rich with anticipation. We believed that life was now and the future and not the past. Of all of us I think it was me who was most impatient for the future. I believed most of what I saw in movies and on TV. Huddled together with El Greco and Bobby over those maps and books, I relished the place names as I scanned the pages: Little Rock, Shoshone, Lake Charles, Detroit, Key West, Milwaukee, San Jose, Buffalo. All of them connecting thoughts in my mind. Girls, guitars, motorcycles, cigarettes, beer.

Ricky Sullivan came into the diner. It was raining, but it was a warm evening, and Ricky looked out of place, shivering in wet clothes, standing by the door, head bowed, looking at us through glazed eyes.

Bobby was the first to speak. He just said, 'Jesus,' then stood up with his milkshake still in his hand, dark brown bubbles sticking to the outside of the glass where he had frothed the chocolate mixture over the rim, blowing hard as hell down the straw as he always did.

Bobby had seen that look before. Bobby saw in Ricky's eyes the same look he had seen in his mother's when she had told him his

117

daddy would not be coming home from church, that he would never be coming home again.

Bobby opened his mouth to speak but nothing came out save a strangled, stuttering, foaming mess. He was starting to look like his milkshake. We stood up from our seats. The rest of the customers carried on with the business of eating hamburgers and ribs and laughing and making love-eyes and getting by. I was stuck on a different plane, mesmerised and frozen by Ricky's haunted eyes. His arms hung loose on his body as he shuffled across the red linoleum towards us. I had never before noticed that the diner had the self-same floor as the barber shop. The same milk chocolate highway of under-layers showing through in the heavy traffic areas, where waitresses walked a million miles carrying trays of instant magic to bulging customers whose belief in the American Dream was symbolised by two pieces of bread stuffed with pickles and burned flesh.

I dropped my burger back on to the tray. Slow motion. Words burst out from the jukebox like shards of exploding steel ripping through the air, tearing through me, saxophone wails bemoaning a loss so deep, so far beyond my understanding. The diner was suddenly an unreal place in an unreal time.

Ricky looked away as though he was searching the hand-painted wall menu for something to order. His voice was soft and quiet and slow as the sound of a jazz ballad opening, of horsehair brushes on a snare drum skin, but I didn't hear a word except for him starting out with, 'It's Jay.'

I didn't say a word. I watched as a collage of images of Pete Obranowicz, Lester Stockton, Joan Taylor and Barbara Felton whizzed across a movie screen in my head, all of them laughing, except Missus Felton, then each of them in death. I had never met

Joan but one day when I called on Old Man Taylor he showed me a photograph of her sitting on a concrete breakwater, smiling into the camera with a beach and waves crashing behind her. He had been sitting on the porch with tears in his eyes, crying unashamedly for his loss, holding the silver frame to his chest.

I thought everyone in there could hear my heart pounding, blood pulsing in my veins, my nerves cracking, sparks flying from my toes and fingertips, my breath sucked into my lungs, throat sealed by steel bands until I felt I had to explode. I ran outside, barging my way through a throng of early-evening diners who were coming in the door. I barely heard the angry words as I burst into the car lot, running fast as I could through the asphalt square, rainwater splashing up my legs as my shoes broke the still reflections below. The shower had been short in duration but heavy in downfall, clearing as quickly as it had begun, and the sky was taking back its summer evening hue. Clouds and soft blue sky smashed into oblivion in mirror pools, where the few remaining faint raindrops had shimmered their image.

I ran so far in the light, warm rain that was all that remained of the downpour that I lost all sense of time and direction, seeking peace and freedom from care and distress and the awful truth: the nakedness of life and death itself. Street names blurred on wooden signs as I pushed through the hurt and into a loose, numb twilight. Courthouse Avenue, Madison Street, Roundway Hill, Van Nuys Avenue. A jumble of names and houses and cars, people and dogs and trees and flags of stripes and stars in the gentle breeze, and none of it made any sense. None of it at all.

Just when I knew I could run forever, I found myself in Cedar Hills, outside the Theodore Roosevelt Memorial Hospital, where

I had kept vigil for El Greco, and later had watched us both on TV.

I stopped on the wide grass lawn that spanned the front of the hospital, a perfect flat expanse of green broken only by the hard black asphalt of the parking lot. The grass was greener than it had ever seemed; emerald and glistening.

Without my noticing it, the rain had stopped, and the air was fresh with warm scents, birds singing their evensong, their call to the ending of the day. As I looked at the front of the hospital, at the double glass doors with the word 'Reception' in green on white, I recalled my mother's words to the starchy nurse the day I had gone to El Greco.

'I am this boy's mother and we would like to see Tony Papadakis.'

I smiled at the memory of that crusty old bitch folding like a pack of cards before my mother's withering gaze.

Recalling the fear I had had back then for El Greco, and his battle, and my mother's private world where she hid her thoughts like love letters in a secret drawer, I resolved to make El Greco's dream come true, and to love life for its own sake as my mother had encouraged me, as my way of freeing her spirit too from its copper cage.

– ELEVEN –

I hurt like hell the day they buried Jay Baglia. His coffin shocked me; it reminded me of a child's pencil box. I had never realised until that day how small he was.

He had so much guts and lust for life that I guess it all camou-flaged him, enveloping him in a huge aura, a teenage Superman. He was always teetering on the edge of reckless, a hand grenade with the pin two-thirds out. That was how he was. He lived a lot of life in a little time. That was how he came to die too, riding his father's motorcycle way too fast out on Wilson Creek Road in the rain. That extra third got Jay Baglia killed. That, and a couple of joints of home-grown pot and three bottles of beer.

Five years older than us, he was the first guy I knew to actually do it. It happened on his fifteenth birthday. Reading from a Spanish phrasebook, he asked his parent's thirty-year-old Puerto Rican housemaid to love him, and she did, every chance she got after that, until his folks came home early one day and caught them at it. His tight-assed mother sent her packing back to Puerto Rico and drove her in tears to the airport to make sure she got on the plane. She said she didn't want any third-world kids in their family.

She had a short memory. Her own grandmother had lived forty years in Brooklyn and couldn't speak more than five words of English when she died, two of which were 'dirty bastard'. But that didn't stop Jay's mom from looking down on immigrants as though they were something unpleasant stuck to her shoe.

Jay's pop took great pleasure in winking at him, and saying, 'Chip off the old block' behind his wife's back after she had exploded that fateful Sunday. He and Jay were both sorry to see Maria go.

His funeral was too much for me. Heartbroken family, distraught friends, and smashed expectations piled on frozen dreams. I hated every minute of it and couldn't wait for it to be over so I could get on with life. Feeling selfish as hell, I choked back tears of rage at a God who had failed again. If he had a school report he would have merited D-minus from me, as an overall assessment, with the epigram 'consistently fails to achieve, must try harder'. It seemed to me I had seen enough death for my brief years, and I wanted a little levity in life. Something to laugh about and blow dark clouds away. To enrich the colours. To shake off the dust.

As though a desperate prayer was answered, the following day marked the start of what was to be a much-needed release: my pop driving us, good as his long-made word, to Savannah, Georgia, where he owned a rental house from which he received a monthly cheque which, as he put it, didn't make him a free man but helped keep me in shoes. I wore out shoes almost as quick as a fat boy eats doughnuts.

His father's sister, who was killed by gardening, had left the house to him. She was a spinster who kept herself to herself, but gardening killed her. She died from pneumonia caught after a fall in her back yard. She broke her hip tripping over a watering can, and lay there helpless as the day she was born until a burglar staking out her property found her and called 911. He only called the ambulance after taking the God-given opportunity to enter her unlocked house and steal a solid silver tea service; the only thing she possessed worth a dime, as my father bitterly put it. Never look a gift horse in the mouth. She was good enough to die when I was really small, so I couldn't remember whether I ever met her at all.

Before we left, El Greco and I wandered up to Old Man Taylor's house, with Bobby in tow. Old Man Taylor wouldn't hear our protestations when he took a small handful of bills out of his battered old wallet, saying, 'Savannah's a fine town, full of history and grace, but it has its expenses just like any other. Just take care, is all.'

He was making the speech about Savannah to distract us from the twenty dollars he was shoving roughly into El Greco's pocket. We knew what his motivation was. Old Man Taylor had adopted us to replace the sons he no longer mentioned. We said our goodbyes as my father pulled up outside Mister Taylor's driveway, the sonorous moan of Mister Felton's old Buick horn calling us to release from the haunting of Jay, his little body still fresh under the newly turned loam.

We hit the Garden State Parkway heading down past Toms River and on towards Atlantic City, hearts light with anticipation and the joy of being alive and free. We had an old transistor radio belting out music into the warm wind that sighed softly around us.

The car radio was broken long before my father got the old car from Mister Felton.

Mister Felton told my father he could have it for being a good friend over the years. He said he didn't have much need for a car where he was going. My pop said he would keep the car in good running order awaiting Mister Felton's release from prison, as a friend would. When Mister Felton was given his reluctant freedom, on appeal by his lawyer who pleaded temporary insanity due to psychological duress which the review judge accepted, reducing his sentence to time served, Mister Felton said he didn't want anything that reminded him of the biggest mistake of his life, and asked my father to keep the car. He wasn't referring to the killing; he simply meant the fact that he'd met and married that parsimonious bitch, Barbara Smith Townsend.

Mister Felton missed the prison library, but he got a job in the public library in Quincy, Boston, close to Merrymount Park and Adams Shore where he loved to walk and look out to the ocean, where his spirit should have been free, but the frozen strands of regret permeated his mind with sudden chills when he thought of the wife who was long since buried but would still not lie down. He loved the city and its bookstores and galleries, and he was close to his beloved Cape Cod, where he fished alone, each Sunday, rain or shine.

We sang along with the radio, tunes we liked and some we didn't. For the ones we disliked we tended to make up new words, taking it in turns to sing verses and choruses, making each one as lewd as we could without my father hearing, oblivious as he was to our whispered huddles in the back. It's truly amazing just how many dirty words you can get into a song if you try real hard.

We broke our journey to eat hot dogs from a stand on the rocky promenade by the beach at Ship Bottom, up from Little Egg Harbor. I had mine as I liked it, double mustard and double ketchup. Like everything else in life I had to consume twice the amount of the things that make life buzz. While my father went to buy the early edition of the newspaper, we chased each other along the sand, laughing under seagull cries and spraying soda that we whipped up in the bottles, thumbs across the tops. Bobby sat on the upturned hull of a small fishing boat watching El Greco and me as we wrote our names in the sand, left damp by the receding tide. I howled with mirth as El Greco wrote 'Lucy Metz loves 69' with his foot, in letters six feet high. Lucy was a prim little girl from our grade class whom El Greco adored. She was pretty as a peach, but her folks were Jehovah's Witnesses, and had brought her up just like them.

Bobby was pensive when we ran back to where he was sitting on the boat. Its hull was rotting, paint peeling from most of its bulk, home now to sand crabs and flies, its wood bleached by wind and sun, just the remains of barnacles clustered on the keel as a reminder of the days it plundered the seas at the rising of the sun, nets cast into the deep green water where fish sang their silent songs for mermaids the fishermen could not see.

'Penny for them?' I said, laughing, afraid that somehow Bobby was going to drag down our sense of fun by referring to his dead father, or to Pete Obranowicz, or worst of all Jay, who was the most recent of the scars that bled in my soul.

'Just thinking about Jay was all.' Bobby sighed, but smiled as he let his breath go. I knew he was thinking of his father, and El Greco, realising this too, grabbed Bobby round the middle, pulling him down on to the soft dry sand, rubbing his face into the yellow grains. Bobby grabbed El Greco by the balloons and said he'd squeeze them dry as a Mormon bar if he didn't let him go. El Greco regarded his sexual organs to be as precious as the gold in Fort Knox, Kentucky, so he let go of Bobby without a second's hesitation.

'You win, Bobby,' he said, making great play of dusting the sand from Bobby's hair and his moonshine face.

I could have stayed there forever on that upturned boat, soaking up the sun and the breeze, the smell of iodine and salt washing through me, making me believe that happiness could last, as the mermaids sang back to the sea. But nothing lasts forever. There were many miles to cross, so many things to see, and the country called out to us in whispers like the mermaids' songs, and like the fishermen, I could hear the songs of the country, strong and clear. They were playing just for me.

My father appeared, newspaper spread in his hands, buffeted by the murmur of breeze, oblivious to our concerns, safe in his grown-up world, where kids did not worry or estimate or plan or assess or contemplate, where men and women thought and children played.

The starter bit and the engine roared lustily, then we were on the road again, sand lifting in our wake as we headed out into the strengthening day, seeking out America.

We stopped at Tuckerton only as long as it took my father to call his office, and for us to turn the T into an F using mud from the roadside; fleeing after taking a picture of Bobby, grinning wildly into the lens of my Polaroid camera as he clung to the town name sign, cracking up with laughter as we all were at what we knew to be genius in action, legends in our own time.

Tuckerton dissolved into New Gretna and Absecon as the old car rolled on. Our excitement was muted now, as this was to be the end of the road for Bobby, who we were to leave with his grand-mother in Margate City, outside of Atlantic City on Absecon Beach. The following day she was to put him on a Greyhound bound for Oceanside, where his mother would collect him. I gave him a candy pig and El Greco gave him five bucks from the money Old Man

Taylor had given us. We messed up his hair and pinched his nose as we said goodbye to him at his grandma's house, my father tooting the old horn as she came down the steps to meet him, beaming with pride at her only daughter's only child. My father picked up the revs and we were gone, down the road so we did not have to suffer a long goodbye. My pop was quite smart sometimes.

– TWELVE –

After leaving Bobby we drove through the seaside dormitory of Ventnor City. Clapboard houses on wood piles, and tin chalets on cinder block supports tumbling along the beach, like so many other towns marking the sand-spit that connected Atlantic City, in broken phrases like Morse code, with Cape May, all the way south on Delaware Bay. Smart little homes with picket fences. Whitewashed or pale lemon, or pink as wedding ribbon, with well-kept gardens, pots or painted cans full to overflowing with geraniums and nasturtiums, all red and orange like flames against the painted walls. Occasionally, like a rotten tooth in an otherwise pearly row, we'd see a peeled old tin shack, roof patched, bitumen weals across its felt, worn car tyres showing cord littering the yard; listless old dog tied to a post, sheltering in shadows from the straining sun. The differing values of their owners stamped upon each home.

We stopped to eat on the outskirts of Atlantic City, parking hard by the kerb in an empty street outside the Hard Luck Diner, probably the most aptly named eatery in America. Nowhere was there a sadder collection of losers with pockets full of empty dreams than here. The Hard Luck was as grey and empty as the lives of the hopeful gamblers who had flocked to Atlantic City to play games of chance in despairing hope of new-found fortune, only to be met by the reinforced certainty that life can sometimes be truly shit, and that hopeful dreaming often produces ever more hopelessness.

I shuddered momentarily and followed El Greco through the screen door into the garish interior, with its Formica-topped tables and posters of baseball stars, the harsh smell of grease and coffee and the sound of eggs popping on the black steel griddle. Joe DiMaggio had acne from being too close to the coffee maker, which sputtered like an old steam engine, defying the laws of obsolescence. We ate slowly. We should have enjoyed this time, in the early afternoon light, as the warm sun kissed the earth and smiled down from its azure sky, but we were laid low by the thoughts we held for Bobby, and the awful burning truth that life would never be the same for any of us.

I pushed eggs and ham around my plate and settled for vanilla coffee, black.

I turned to El Greco and stared absently at him, as my father sat away up at the counter, having got himself into a sports conversation with the owner, a dusty-looking red-faced man who reminded me of Elmer Fudd.

'These are strange times, Tony,' I said. 'I don't know what anything means any more, can't make much sense of it all. You know what I mean?'

My voice cracked with emotion as I said his real name, which I rarely used when we were alone in our closed and secret world.

'Ain't nothing going to be the same,' he replied. 'High school and then who knows what? You just have to make the most of it, whatever comes your way. You just have to go out and get it, don't wait for it to come to you. Look at these folks. Not a goddamned one of them ever went out and got a goddamned thing by the look of 'em. Living on dreams, just like my dear old dad. I hope that bastard's lying dead somewhere, deep in the ground.'

He paused, looked out of the window as though something out

there was calling him, and added, 'I hope that bastard's test was big.'

His words bounced against the dusty window and floated out like slow shrapnel into my burning face. I don't know why I felt so melancholy; maybe it was Jay and Bobby, and Bobby's father, and Bobby's mom who would never let him go any further than Margate City, scared to death that he too would leave her, scared that when her own mother died she would be as alone in this world as anyone can be. And there was El Greco, old before his time, chewed up inside over his daddy, figuring everybody had some test in life. What he meant I couldn't say, but all the time I had the sense that he knew, and that it was to do with his destiny, and mine too, all caught up together.

We left my father to pay the dead-eyed waitress, and without speaking, without a word of thanks, we floated out into the street. Two supernatural beings in an unreal town in an unreal world. We took our places on the bonnet of the old car, feeling the heat of the sun pulsing in rhythm to our easy breathing as we thought our thoughts of sorrow and freedom.

I wondered about life and its collage of events, its joys and its dark, hideous schemes. Pete Obranowicz and Jay Baglia and Missus Felton and Bobby's father, all in their holes in the ground, to be eaten by worms and time. Mister Barr and his hateful view of education. Mister Schwartz and his uneasy love of us. Old Man Taylor who replaced his sons with us. Mister Felton and his tenderness and love of books, but then again, a man who could kill. Maybe it was all gone.

The air grew hazy around me and I had that sense of slipping through time again, when my mind tripped out and images materialised through my thoughts the way hot coffee falls slowly through filter paper. I looked across the street towards the Shamrock Bar and Grill, and ten years rolled by, driven by the breeze. Bobby rolled out of the cracked old bar, stuffing his shirt into his pants, swaggering as he walked. Twenty-two years old. He turned slightly as his boots banged on the wooden steps, and waved almost imperceptibly to a dark-eyed girl as she smiled slyly down at him from the balcony window. She blew him a great big kiss, the size of Texas, and she was gone.

I let my eyes snap shut and open again. In whipped reality, and I was back with El Greco, on the fender of Mister Felton's solid old car, the Hard Luck Diner still across from us. El Greco opened his mouth to make some wisecrack, but thought better of it, and rolled his eyes skywards instead, content to let the moment hang.

My father came out of the diner, whistling some old tune, shielding his eyes from the sun, acclimatising; then he was up by the car, keys in hand, ruffling El Greco's hair and then mine in turn. We took our seats without a word, then eased out into the street, bonded in our solitude.

Before we left for the trip El Greco and I had tried to persuade Bobby that the adventure was there for us all, our dream of a road trip, even though it would be supervised by my father, but in our hearts we knew that Bobby could never shake off that greatest of all responsibilities: the love of his mother. In truth we didn't try too hard. We had left him outside his grandma's house, with his broad smile and his waving arm, cap in hand, as we sped off, tooting the horn, fractured in a trail of dust and half-remembered and half-forgotten promises. For some reason, indefinable to me then, deep, bloody gashes were left in my soul by the temporary loss of a friend, and the ending of a time of innocence.

'No more downs, let's live a little,' I said to El Greco, slipping back into the moment, suddenly lifted as he raised his hand, thumb up. As if sensing our need to break away, my pop stepped on the gas and the solid old Buick kicked up a notch, the low rumble of its engine raising pitch as though it too was keen for the road. We hit the edge of town, the boardwalk lost from sight behind towering casinos and block hotels, and my father pointed the fender south on the highway, aimed straight at the Carolinas.

El Greco and I banged soda bottles together, the click of glass sharp and bright in the confines of the interior, as air whooshed past the open windows. 'Here's to Bobby Stockton!' yelled El Greco out of the window to the listening world, where the earth sighed and Callery pear trees swayed, a thousand cheerleaders with the sound turned down.

'Bobby Stockton!' I shouted, eyes wild and radiant.

'King of New Jersey!' cried El Greco.

The sound of glass on glass. We laughed at the world, and the world laughed back. The road was ours, stretching into the distance as though the prairie railroads of Saskatchewan were laid before us, straight and strong in reassurance, the beating heart of the world.

I no longer recall the trail of thoughts that ribboned in the warm wind behind us, lost in that frozen frame of life that passed us by then quietly dissolved, the present becoming the past.

The sun hung high behind us in an incandescent sky, as clumps of pines and hickory slid away. Green and grey-green and black. The earth was browning now, the heat of summer stripping green from the land, warming the landscape in shades of ochre, burnt umber, and flax.

I watched smoke fall from my father's nostrils, mouth closed in pensive silent appraisal of the scene before him, when suddenly he smiled beatifically to himself and eased back into the worn seat, as comfortable as his mother's womb. I asked him what he was thinking of, and he smiled to himself again, and without looking my way said, 'Oh, just about your mom, and about times long gone by, and about when you were born. Did she ever tell you that you were premature? Three weeks early and small as a dove, but you sure got big quick. Never saw a child grow as quick as you. Never been on time since either.'

Then he laughed to himself again and, completely unlike him, hit the horn, sending a cloud of quail up from the scrub and thorns, and El Greco popped at them with a silent shotgun, then they were gone, the landscape as still again as a mirrored lake.

We stopped for gas at a no-name hamlet with little white houses and lawns as neat as cemeteries, the whole place wrapped in a sleepiness that hid the turmoil of life and loves and the bittersweet relationships that happen everywhere, that no amount of chasing or running away from can avoid. The proprietor was a gritty-looking man dressed in faded dungarees, with a short-brimmed hat that one time had had *Exxon* printed on the front, but now said *xon*, from where he fingered the front with hands greased and grained from years of tender care of engines that spoke to him in a language he understood.

I looked him in the eye, but saw nothing: no hint of joy or pain, of love or emptiness, just the passing of time, with no particular story to be seen, or perhaps none to tell. Or so many tales layered one on top of the other that their weight, like the cover of a great book, hid his stories from view, and from the scrutiny and intrusion of a passing stranger, who had no real business to be looking. I felt a pressing need to ask his story, but let it pass for fear of intruding where I was not welcome, and also from the fear that there might be nothing to hear, that all he possessed was emptiness. He pumped the gas as he had a million times and took our bills. He bid us good day, and turned his back, touching his hat as he went, an unconscious habit born out of the repetition of a hundred thousand experiences, each similar, but with a unique strand, like the chain of genes that makes us each individual despite our similarities of purpose and design.

My pop sat contentedly at the wheel, relaxed, smoke drifting up in lazy spirals towards the half-open window, where suddenly it was sucked silently away, as though dragged by unseen hands. The old Buick ate up the miles, a quiet diner in a peaceful land, easy with the calm that cotton farmers make their own.

'Jay would have loved this,' I said to El Greco, expecting no response and getting none, save the wistful smile that was answer enough and removed the need for words. El Greco smiled a lot in that dreamy way. My own mind was always crashing in tight circles, a mesh of cogs and gears, as though driving some great machine that had no function, but El Greco carried serenity in smooth pools with sandbars between each one, so there was resource and the possibility of transfer, without everything being held in one great sea. I envied him.

El Greco and I were up front now, sitting on the great bench seat with my father. I kicked off my shoes and placed my feet up on the dash and daydreamed my way through a series of small towns with names that meant nothing to me. Clermont. Swainton. Burleigh. I never questioned what caused the builders of those places to give them their names. I had no right to ignore them because I was in search of America and it was my duty to seek out the reason and the history of each and every one. Then we were at Cape May, on to the car ferry with its oversized funnel, bands of green and Indian gold, then across Delaware Bay and into the state of Delaware and the little town of Lewes, which barely registered as we headed south once more.

My father suddenly pulled the old car on to the baked earth at the side of the highway, and swung it back the way we had come, clouds of red-grey dust rising as we turned. 'Just fancied a beer,' he said slyly, as we parked outside a fresh-painted diner that had four giggly girls drinking soda at a bench outside.

I laughed, knowing that our chances were less than zero, but worth taking just the same, breaking out of the melancholy that had resettled on us uninvited.

Their names were Gail, Honey, Jenny and Bobbie-Sue, or some such things. Apple pie and ice-cream. Their talk would be of movie stars, like girls their age the nation through. The owner, staring out from behind the fine screen door, gave El Greco and me a scathing look as we perched ourselves on the bench down from the girls even though all the other varnished seats were free. Maybe one was his daughter – who knew, and, more to the point, who really cared. Not us, that was for sure; we were too young. He knew we were passing through, and he would be glad to see us go. One beer, two roots and gone. Just fine with him.

I wondered about his story too, but I could see from the rattlesnake eyes, and the corroded corners of his spiteful mouth, that here lay only a tale of resentment and lost life that would reveal nothing but negatives; a story that should never be told.

We lied to the girls and told them we were on our way to LA to screen-test for a movie about two boys trapped in a haunted house with a woman who was supposed to be their aunt, but who turned out to be an impostor who had escaped from an asylum, murdered their real aunt, and buried her in the pumpkin patch. They pretended to accept this, but none of us really believed this fabrication. We were great liars, but things had shifted a little for us, and our hearts were not really in it. Still, it was fun, and El Greco made them laugh with his Goofy impression and I did mine of Mickey Mouse calling 'Pluto'. They were nice kids, and I hoped that none of them had that mean old bastard for a father.

El Greco and I waved jauntily as we drove out on to the highway, tyres hissing on the rippled concrete road. As we rolled south, I wondered about Bobby, thinking of his mother, who needed him to replace his father when she should have left him free. I pondered the possibility that it was Bobby who did not allow his own freedom, that he needed that jolly, fragile woman as much as she needed him, and maybe more so. Bobby was good and honest in a way I didn't even aspire to. Some people believe they truly are, but very few have such entrenched purity, immune from self-parody and tricks of the soul. Self-image and promotion were not in Bobby's repertoire. Bobby Stockton was the rare kind of kid you could ask to chaperone your sister, knowing that he was the one at risk. He certainly would have been at risk with my sister, if the arguments she had with my folks were anything to go by; her not being trusted to be left alone with boys and all. Even when he did something he shouldn't have done, dragged in by El Greco and me, he didn't boast about it the way I would have done, all swelling chest and cockerel crowing, prancing and preening, strutting and seeking out of fame and recognition. He didn't get sucked in too often. Bobby knew where responsibility and opportunity took different roads. He was seldom in two minds about which to walk. Me, now, I was a different case in point. Opportunity and responsibility were blurred cousins, not so well known to each other, and difficult to define. Sure, I knew wrong from right on any given day, but I chose to shave their edges or give their make-up a little smudge to blur the glints of truth that shone out at me; a little something to spice up a day that might have been tending towards mediocrity. I found small comfort in the thought that at least I wasn't a nymphomaniac like Lauren or Joe Baglia's housemaid Maria. I knew Lauren was a 'cause for exasperation' because I heard my mom tell someone on the telephone that she was. After the kissing thing died down she persuaded my folks to let her go for a camping weekend with her best friend Dora Fredericks. Dora was Methodist and her parents were real devout, so my folks agreed and off they went on their bicycles to Canyon Lake with one two-man tent. Turned out the Hahn brothers took their two-man tent along too. Dora Fredericks wasn't nearly as devout as her folks. Neither was Lauren.

I let thoughts of Bobby evaporate into the yearning sky as the old car ate up the miles without complaint, the big engine throbbing easily, a mess of oil and steel and pistons and gears. Mister Felton had treated that car with a whole lot more love than he ever received from his wife. He serviced it every three thousand miles or three months, whichever came first, as he was so fond of saying. It was regular as clockwork. Mister Felton never did more than a hundred miles a week, except for his occasional trips to Cape Cod where he loved to stand and stare at the ocean, and dream of a happiness he could not define. The oil-changes and greased bearings had made the car good despite its years, and I thought kindly of Mister Felton as we rolled steadily south. It didn't feel like a murderer's car. It felt quiet and steady and warm, just as Mister Felton had always been, until the day he snapped.

Delaware in all its softness dissolved into Maryland, proving that the political lines of state boundaries and nation states alike were the constructions of man. As my pop said, a line on a map was just that. A strong man could draw a new line on it just as easily as a weak man might help him to erase the old, and the memory of its existence. He got that from his pop, who knew a thing or two about just about everything.

We drove through Maryland with the same blurred reality that adventure thrives on, diverting slightly to catch sight of the Atlantic Ocean and Assateague Island in the distance. Hump-backed sand dunes and marsh grass saved the coastlands from the threatening sea, watched overall by a white-and-red-hooped lighthouse, glorious, emphasising the solitude of that beautiful and lonely place.

Peace descended on us like birds, sunlight fading above the dark cypress swamps along the Pocomoke River in soft hues of violet and cornflower.

We fell across the small town of Snow Hill twenty miles out from Ocean City with its charming old houses and few signs of change to disturb its founders. My father took a room in a farmhouse, allowing El Greco and me to pass an easy night in our two-man tent, sleeping with the canopy doors tied back, watching the glittering stars in the night sky, blacker than an Ivory Coast shaman, and huge, so immense that I marvelled and struggled to comprehend the enormity of it all. I tried to talk to El Greco about how I couldn't deal with the idea of infinity, of a world and a universe created by a God I didn't know, so I asked him who created God, but he just smiled at me and handed me a fresh cigarette, and that was, in that moment, all I needed to know. I lay on my front, propped on my elbows as I stared straight across the black field, and down the curving hill at the stars in front of me; cigarette smoke curling away blue with moonlight, rising at first, then drifting down from the sharp pricked lights towards the shimmering silvered oil of the lazy river.

We rose early, eager and hungry. Fresh farm eggs, ham as thick as the plates themselves, black coffee rewarded by a grinning shrug from my pop to the farmer's wife. Then we were over Chesapeake Bay and the tunnels and bridges and causeways that seemed to stretch for ever in an eighteen-mile line and into the town of Norfolk, Virginia, with its bustle of cranes and construction and traffic noise, and everywhere the evidence of government. General Douglas MacArthur lay quiet and dead, memorialised along with his 1950 Chrysler Imperial, as we pushed on through that town.

We beat down through the Dismal Swamp with its decayed beauty, dark clumps of cypress and juniper, and the aroma of honeysuckle lying heavy and sticky across the air. Swamp water like pools of oil, black and mirrored, watched over by buzzards circling high on thermals invisible as gas.

I was daydreaming of the Carolinas; then, as if my dream was granted, we were down and through Elizabeth City, across Albemarle Sound and over that sheet of river into the town of Williamston, and on down 17, over the Tar River at the west edge of Pamlico Sound with its bounded shores; pines and wild oaks scattered like confetti. We passed by sleepy odd-named hamlets; Chocowinity, Wilmar, Ernul, skirting the Croatian Forest, and Catfish Lake in its swampy hole. Country blurred into town and the outskirts of Jacksonville, North Carolina, home to the US Marine Corps, but the restless Buick purred on down through Verona, Folkestone, Hampstead and on to Wilmington, where my pop suddenly said, 'Enough is enough,' and pulled the wheel hard over and rolled into the lot of a fine-looking diner set back from the highway, flanked by trees, tall pines heavy with wealth.

We had covered hundreds of miles without incident or adventure, but the sense of anticipation was on our nerve-ends and it sparked and crackled in the evening air. 'Rooms For Rent', so the sign said at the side of Fat Chester's Diner. My pop parked the car out front, came out two minutes later and told us to haul our things inside.

The proprietor of Fat Chester's had a sense of humour characterised by the diner's name. Fat Chester was about the thinnest man I ever saw. Arms as slight as chair spindles extended from his crisp white shirt, the half-sleeves creased to perfection, straight as a Texas highway.

Chester had an easy smile, wide as a bridge. His was a simple story. He had given up on the rush of New York City, selling insurance to people who mostly didn't need it, much like Forest Johnson, making his deadlines and watching his month-on-month targets rise, but not his pay. So he had cashed in some policies of his own, loaded up his station wagon with his family and a mongrel dog named Diablo and headed south, chancing destiny.

He had put all his savings in the diner and never looked back. His wife and kids were happy, and even Diablo – rust, mustard, white, black and old though he was – appeared content as he lay in the recess of the porch steps, tail flicking idly as he eyed the slow-turning world.

We ate a dinner of the sweetest, most tender ribs I ever tasted, better even than Oceanside's Barbecue King's, served with bucket-sized scoops of home-made coleslaw and red cabbage salad, then excused ourselves, leaving my father with Chester. I heard his voice floating through the open window and out through the screen, railing against the decline in moral standards, his well-worn views receiving warm support from Fat Chester, who had long considered the country gone to hell if the power of religion should ever be diluted, as though the Antichrist was in the very next street, just waiting his turn.

We sauntered slowly in the heavy evening air, hands in pockets, no real cares to chase away. Pear-like fruit the colour of copper pennies hung in clusters from the thin, bowed branches of some foreign-looking tree that guarded the driveway to a smart blue-roofed house with little twisted turrets, like turbans, at each gable end. They gave it the appearance of being Russian, or so El Greco said, and I agreed, not knowing what a Russian house looked like, and not wanting to appear dumb. We headed into a small park, well kept and orderly, where a group of black kids played softball with a home-stitched ball, away from the baseball diamond where smart-kitted white kids with regulation hair and professional catcher's mitts played with zeal, all straining to win, little pleasure evident in their tight, tanned faces. We sat on the grass a little way off from the softball players, who watched us coyly, sly eyes cast across us as though searching for something beyond us.

El Greco rucked up his jeans leg and pulled a pack of Kents from his sock, his usual hiding place, and passed one to me. He struck a loose match on a piece of stone, and smoke burst into the air as sulphur flared. I leaned in, drew long and hard and exhaled, the evening suddenly thick with smoke that hung uneasily for a moment, then drifted upwards.

I lay half on my back, elbow propping me up so I could watch their game, smoking like a sultan gazing over his harem, or a nightclub manager observing his clientele. All the time I had the sense that they were watching me as much as I watched them, their studied indifference suddenly thrown into disarray as their ball, well struck by an athletic-looking boy whose wide-gapped teeth reminded me of a picket fence, flew high and wide towards us.

The ball dropped short and rolled up to my leg, bouncing back as it struck my shin.

They stood there, fixed to their positions as though glue bonded them to the grass. El Greco stood up slowly, stooped, picked up the ball and held it out for the nearest boy to take. But a strange thing happened. He stayed where he was, making no attempt to take back the ball.

I looked at him, as if for the first time, at his khaki shorts, pulled in at the waist, with great handfuls of material gathered in front, like ballroom curtains held shut with a kilt pin, the colour long since faded from repeated washing and the friction of hand-held soap. His pressed T-shirt was straight out of the fifties, once white, now grey with age. His shoes were canvas, too small, so someone had cut a section from the front. A big toe poked out from each one. He was about eight years old, but looked older. His lean face burned copper in the lowering sun.

'It's okay. Take the ball.'

El Greco stood where he was, his words unanswered, and still they stood there, looking from one to the other, back at El Greco, and then to me, as if to see what trick we were up to. Then I stood up, took the few short paces to El Greco's side, removed the ball from his hand, walked up to the boy and held the ball out to him. He hesitated, looking from the ball to me and back again.

I spoke softly. 'Go on, take it.'

He looked at me fearfully, still sly-eyed. It was like nothing I ever saw before, worse even than the doleful eyes of a run-down dog I discovered on Roundway Hill one morning as I walked to school. The dog had been hit by a vehicle that had driven on. Pain, surprise and desperation mixed like paints on an artist's palette in those eyes, and that look haunted me for days. The mistrust in this boy's eyes reminded me of that dog, but here was a look that bewildered me, for I had never seen such hopelessness silently expressed, not even in Mister Felton's eyes the day he killed Barbara.

Time paused that evening, like a scene snapped in the flash from a giant camera, the park frozen in a weird image where we all stood still but a man in the distance walked his dog and the white kids threw and struck and ran, as though two scenes were laid over each other, one animated, the other motionless, a fragment of time passed by.

I started to feel foolish, hand held out, naked, exposed, and a little anger rose in me. 'Just take the ball.' My words sounded harsh and metallic, ringing the way announcements clatter around the subways in New York City. I added, 'Please?' as an after-thought, and the boy gingerly extended his hand and took the ball from mine.

'You ain't from roun' here, are y'all?' he asked in a slow, deliberate voice; quiet but strong, and deeper than his look gave expectation of.

'No, we're not,' I answered simply.

The boy turned to walk away, as the others drifted towards the shrubbery, then spun his head quickly and said, 'Thank you,' his words almost inaudible against a sudden burst of noise from the baseball players, disputing a three-strike call.

El Greco and I stood watching them make their way up through the clusters of dogwood, elder and mimosa, and then they were gone, out through a repaired but recut hole in the chainlink fence, and down towards a group of prefabricated houses, bolted concrete sheets making one-storey homes of equal dimensions, each in identical-sized lots in a tiny trailer park, overshadowed by a brick warehouse, its windows now shards of jagged glass, panes long since broken in.

I looked across to the side of the park, to the gate we had entered by, and there were the single-storey ranch-style houses, and two-storey wood-fronted homes with wide porches, wisteria and ivy-grown as prosperous as a milk farm cat.

El Greco walked slowly over to the dry earth of the shrubbery, where the base of the bushes sat in circular indentations. Park gardeners hose-sprayed those shrubs each morning, except for those humid days when banging summer rain had fallen in lines like uncoiled solder through the heavy southern night.

I followed him as I always did, curious and not a little apprehensive. I had never been to a black area before, excepting when we drove up through Newark by the throughway, or up through Harlem and the Bronx, and then we were like movie-goers, watching a scene as it passed us by. We had been bussed on a school visit to Woodlawn Cemetery to see the grave of Herman Melville who wrote *Moby-Dick*, because Miss Anderson was crazy about *Moby-Dick*. I wasn't that fussed about whales and all, big though they were. But Tony was crazy excited about *Moby-Dick*. Nearly as crazy as Miss Anderson. He was crazy about anything to do with the ocean.

There were only a handful of black kids in Oceanside, the children of successful middle-management types like Forest Johnson who was the exception that proved the rule. The further south we had come, the more shacks we had seen: tarpaper and tin-sheet huts by the roadsides and in the fields, and the people staring out from the gloom into the sunlight, white-eyed and watchful. I had felt a strange unease at the sight of people walking without shoes, something I did often in the yard or on the beach, but never would have done in a field of snakes, or on the burning sheen of a hard asphalt road.

El Greco made his way up the well-worn path to the fence, and I got closer, caught between the desire to go back to the safe belly of Fat Chester's, and the need to be there with him. I knew that irrespective of the outcome I'd be right with El Greco, despite the cautioning voice loud inside my head that saw, as ever, the folly this could lead to. He turned to look at me, smiling his reassuring smile, the one that always worked with me no matter what we were intending. It was like looking in the mirror. I used to practise looks a lot. Looking tough. Looking cool. Looking sexy. Looking mad. Looking like Humphrey Bogart. Looking like Keith Richards. Looking like Elvis. Looking like my hero Robert Mitchum. Looking like my father. Looking like Adolf.

El Greco lifted up the torn tangle of new chainlink, pushing it against the old rusted fence with its sharp brown ends, then we were through and out the other side. That simple act felt like something huge, something indefinable, like being on a tour of the White House and slipping into the Oval Office unnoticed and going through the President's desk. Or with your friends going through their mother's underwear drawer while their folks were at church. That kind of something huge.

Although the sun was still in the sky, shadows were lengthening in slick dark bands like sump oil draining. I followed El Greco down the dry mud slope, all red-brown and cracked as though someone had stamped terracotta tiles into the earth, haphazard and drunken. The kids we had followed were nowhere to be seen. A ghostly quiet lay over the trailer park, broken only by the muffled sound of canned laughter on an early evening television show, probably *I Love Lucy* or *Mister Ed*.

I saw no one as we measured our steps down the slope, save for an old black man on a porch, stock still in his rocking chair, old briar pipe, smokeless, hanging between his lips. He was cut in two by shadow, his worn grey trousers, button-fly strained by his bowed-out legs, stark clear in the lowering sunlight and hued with pink, while his pea-green shirt and weather-creased face were made the darker for the contrast. He eyed us easily, for close to the end of his years a man has nothing to fear but death itself. We walked down towards him for lack of any other focal point and as we did I flashed through newsreel, Martin Luther King Jr. shot at the Lorraine Hotel, Memphis on April 4th, just over two years ago, and the day after telling the congregation at Bishop Mason Temple, 'I've been to the mountaintop... and I've looked over, and I've seen the Promised Land', and then he added, as though he saw the assassin's bullet spiralling and hissing through the air, 'I'm not fearing any man. Mine eyes have seen the glory of the coming of the Lord.'

My guess is he saw the Lord a little sooner than he was banking on.

El Greco stood facing the porch where the old man had begun rocking slowly as though unseen breezes had caught him like a sail. Hands thrust in pockets as ever, bold as brass, he said, 'Howdy!'

The old man stared at El Greco, then at me, then back to El Greco, and lifted his hand slowly and said, 'Howdy do.'

It was a kind of fair exchange. Nothing really given away, and nothing received. Or so momentous that all that was needed to express the enormity of our difference in birth and opportunity was the exchange of a greeting. Either way we all nodded, and the old man touched the brim of his flat cloth cap and El Greco and I walked slowly across the flagstones, weeds standing still as a bird dog.

Almost every prefab house had a heap of junk to the side. Old tyres, some laid two or three in a pile and filled with soil, flowers growing out; broken chairs, one or two legs missing; deckchairs with the canvas torn like ripped shirts; tin baths, holed and rusty; old refrigerators, doors hanging off. Every conceivable domestic and motor-related appliance was here, the great domestic and auto breakers' yard of the world. Each decayed item, each broken part representing hope or desperation, depending on your view. These were people with very little, and the more I saw, the less there was to see.

I looked around the trailer park at the orderly lots, and every-where was the evidence of decay. Tricycles with three distinct and different wheels, basketball rings made from beer barrel hoops, television aerials made out of strips of fencing wire, door knockers contrived from brass cupboard handles, house nameplates made from sheets of Formica tabletop, sawed down and painted with names so fancy they evoked honey-and-milk-soaked country. Roseheath, Merrymount, Dahlia, Cherryvale. A battered sky-blue Cutlass, hubcaps from Ford, Buick, Dodge and Chevrolet, fender by Chrysler of Detroit. Washed clothes hanging from a line of discarded ropes, desperate in their stitched and re-stitched repair, and patched together like survivors of some immense combat, some battle so intense that no one would mention its name. Baby buggies made from old wood crates set in abandoned dolly wheels, and lined with old curtains, handles made from cut and beaten cooper's iron. A child's cart created from a cement-splashed builder's plank, an orange box with 'Florida Sunkist' burned in the wood, buggy wheels at the front, buckle-spoked bicycle wheels to the rear. In one trailer the American flag over the window for a curtain, and in another 'Pop's Market – Open Late Nite', while in others shards of cloth of every shade, remnant pieces of psyche-delic colours sold for twenty-five cents a yard in the reductions at Sears, stitched at the top to form a tube through which ran stiff plastic-coated wire, fixed to a nail at either end. Television sets salvaged from the back lots of midtown bars, and repaired with the guts of similar junk, or stolen by means of burglary, or purchased second-hand from Drummer's pawn shop. Interfer-ence-spoiled pictures dusted with early evening snow, and turned up loud, hissing. And everywhere the muted sound of women calling their menfolk to eat, their calls met by the low rumble of tired working voices. Children calling. Names. Drinks. Food.

The hum of life itself, and all of it a mystery to me. I felt eyes upon me, although I could see no faces. I looked around at the old man, a way behind us now, rocking slowly; still at anchor, insufficient wind to carry him off, sat waiting to sail another sea.

We crossed through the trailer park, cloak shadows thrown across it now by the warehouse. An old blind dog barked at us, tail waving as it itched around on the spot, keen to run to us, experience telling it to stay put, to jig around on that spot safe from kicks and cars. I pitched a piece of wood at it, teasing it to chase what it could not see, and immediately I thought of the orphan kids from the home in Oceanside and felt bad to the bone. El Greco shot me one of his old-man looks, so I smirked at him, as though to say, 'I know, I know.'

Out from the trailer park, we crossed through the bay of Bubba's Gas Station with its broken concrete forecourt, old tyres piled high against the side of the store, and more stacked by the body shop which advertised 'Oil Changed – Cheep'. I snickered to myself and said, 'Guess the mechanics here are just chicken.'

El Greco laughed. 'Wonder if the batteries are fitted by hens?'

Then he added, sombre as night, 'Most of these people probably didn't have any real schooling. It's no surprise they don't spell too well.'

My father hated bad spelling and poor grammar. I heard him one day talking to Mister Schwartz and he said if the government didn't do something about advertising real soon, the kids in the country would actually think that easy was spelt E-Z-Y, and that night was N-I-T-E. He said the country was going to rat-shit, and pretty soon the concept of the newspaper would be redundant because nobody would be able to read. He was always exaggerating, but Mister Schwartz agreed with him, just to get along. We had seen the grave of Joseph Pulitzer along with Herman Melville on our visit to Woodlawn Cemetery. Joseph Pulitzer. Newspaper magnate. El Greco knew who he was. Tony Papadakis knew something about everything, just like my pop's father. If he wasn't laid down there Mister Pulitzer would no doubt have been banging on with my father about the nation's crippled intellect. He died down in Charleston on October 29th 1911, so how he got to be buried in New York was anybody's guess.

The ancient pumps stood to attention, nozzles high up in their casings, looking for all the world like soldiers saluting, their dials all at different readings, pointers at varying degrees like clocks which stopped at different times as though marking momentous events, or simply refusing to tick again.

I looked hard at the front of Bubba's. Somebody had worked long to make it look more than it was. The cash office and body shop were made of pressed tin sheets, bolted together and painted dark green, the colour of park railings. The signs were all home-made: chipped and weathered now but painted by a steady, patient hand. The panes of glass in the cash-room door varied, most no-ticeably around the lock, where countless generations of teenage burglars had broken in. Hubcaps of every type were nailed in banks above the body shop door, the whole array towered over by a set of the biggest cow horns I ever saw. The roof was bolted on: sheets of corrugated plastic, once clear as water but yellowed now, and green-stained by moss that clung around the studs.

I imagined Bubba to be a kindly giant of a man with wire-wool hair and a round, jovial face, creased in a permanent smile.

A reversible sign set in a concrete base on the edge of the forecourt displayed a simple fact. 'CLOSED'.

We walked on over the street towards a row of hopeful shops selling nickel goods, and a café, whose chalkboard offered the day's special. Red beans and rice with crawfish gumbo. Sounded good.

There were people about here, standing on street corners, talking, or pushing home-made buggies like those in the trailer park. All of them black. An old man in denim dungarees and rubber sandals, the kind kids wear, sat on the porch outside a boarded-up store which had the name, 'Wilmington Cook Supplies', in faded white letters on black across the weatherboard. As though the place could be anything else, someone had painted

'Closed 4 Bizness' across the heavy nailed boards. Joseph Pulitzer and my father would have had plenty to say about that.

Everyone there watched us pass. Not one of them said a word to us, and, when I looked at them, they looked back for a half-second at most, then averted their eyes. Something I was getting used to.

We carried on up the street. Impossible as it seemed, things got poorer. Mainly boarded-up stores, and at the intersection of Main Street and No Name Street a brazier made from an oil drum with punched-in holes; charcoal burned and glowed beneath a heavy iron plate on which sat pecan nuts, salted and roasting. The vendor, blind and ragged as torn paper, held a scoop in one hand and sheets of newspaper in the other. El Greco and I walked up to him, and as we got close he said, 'Salt pecans? Only one nickel the scoop.'

He was the first person to speak a word to us since the old man, and I guess I was longing to say something, so I said, 'I'll take a scoop.'

Deft from years of practice, he turned the piece of newspaper into a cone quicker than the eye could see, and almost at the same instant he had the scoop into the middle of the nuts and was up through them and, practice-perfect, letting the smoking nuts fall against the inside of the paper, not a fraction off course.

'Little lost, ain't ya, fellas?' he said quietly.

'Just looking around is all,' I said, suddenly afraid that a blind man could see the colour of my skin from the sound of my voice, and thought fit to warn us off.

'Don' min' me sayin', but this ain't no place for no white folks. Only white folks that ever comes roun' here is the po-leece, an' then ain't no good thing, no way.'

151

He whistled as he spoke, on account of a gap in his teeth where a tooth had fallen out, probably knocked out by someone who didn't like his nuts. I took the cone from him, thanked him, and paid him a dime, to which he told me I'd overpaid him, giving me the chance to say what I'd always wanted to. 'Keep the change.'

'Don' min' if ah do, yessir.'

El Greco had walked on, making me trot to catch him up. He knew if he'd stayed at the old man's stand I would have been pushing to get out of there, but as usual he wanted to go further into the pie, licking his lips for just one more small slice. I offered him the cone. He took a fistful of nuts, chewed them, and declined my second offer. 'Too much salt.'

We had turned west from the vendor's corner into a smaller street. Weed-grown lots spaced between the poorest homes I ever saw. Rotten timber-framed shacks with plastic sheets held down by house bricks to keep rainwater from seeping through holes in the tarpaper roofs. Sagging porches, rat holes gnawed through. A group of children playing together on a mound of dried mud. Discarded trash in old boxes by the sidewalks. No regular refuse collection here.

I was scared and I didn't much care if El Greco knew it. I was about to suggest we get the hell out of there when the sounds of angry drunken shouting juddered across the evening like machine-gun fire in an amusement arcade. I spun around to face the sounds and saw a shabby wooden building across the narrow street. The word 'BAR', hand-painted on a barrel-top hanging from a nail in the board wall, was the sole announcement of purpose. Not 'Lucky's Bar' or 'Frank's Bar and Grill'. Just 'BAR'.

Perfunctory. Beer. Gin. Bourbon. Scotch maybe. Definitely no vermouth.

I stood stock-still. Scared.

The angry voices got angrier. Louder. Then the staccato yells of other voices. Panicky frightened voices.

Suddenly the door burst open and out into the street, not thirty feet from where we stood, came two young black men, one staggering backwards, hand to his neck, blood pouring red through his fingers and down to the dry dirt. The second man, eyes bulging wide in their sockets, nostrils flared, knife in hand, lunged forward at him and suddenly, with frightening speed, he was astride the bleeding man on the ground, as though I had shut my eyes or someone had cut part of the scene from a roll of film, and was stabbing at him, grunting with the effort of it, face shiny with sweat as though he had just run a race.

The sound of thunder suddenly hammered on the air. Pulverising waves of noise thudded against the buildings and crashed back again, rattling glass in frames and calling the whole world to order with a woeful and vengeful fury.

I saw the gunman then, both arms raised in the shadowed doorway of the little bar. He was holding the biggest handgun I had ever seen, bigger still as this was real. No cameras. No lights.

The stabber was blown forward, mid-stab. He toppled into the dirt, blood sawing out from his back, guts spinning out front. He lay still as a chameleon, gun cry still rocking back and forth. I expected to see a flash of lightning, but there was none. The sound still rolled moaning like sea behind a harbour wall as the gunman stepped up to the knifeman, shot him again, as if to make sure the dead man did not come back to life, and shouted angrily, 'I dun tol' you stay away from my brother!'

He took his brother's hand, gently pulled up the bleeding youth and quickly they were gone, out of sight into an alleyway. I turned towards the bar, expecting to see a crowd of dazed and curious onlookers as there had been when Missus Felton had got what was coming to her, but there was no one. Not a soul. The 'BAR' sign was gone, and the door closed tight as though it had never been.

El Greco and I stood together, staring straight at the dead man, a dark pool now by his stomach, and another where most of his head had been.

A siren suddenly cut the night, mournful and absolute. We stood still, as though our feet had grown from the ground, as though we had always been there, as at one with the earth as the lime tree in the vacant lot across the street.

I don't know why, but I started eating the salt pecans, still warm in the paper cone. Then I offered them to El Greco and without saying a word he took some.

The siren, loud now, smothered the air.

I heard a call, indistinct against the siren wail. I looked up the street to see the pecan seller, his hand raised as though he sensed us there, knowing we were the only ones with nowhere to hide. We drifted over to where he stood, a short way from his brazier.

A police car pulled up short of the body and two cops got out, guns in hand, doors left open. One walked across to the dead man, shook his head and looked around him, gun pointing still at the body, as though telling its own story. *Trust no one. They may not be dead.* His partner strode across to us, shaking his head and squinting as though there was something wrong with the picture, but he could not quite work it out.

'For Christ's name's sake, what in the hell are you kids doing here?'

'Well, officer suh, they was jis' buyin' some o' ma mighty fine nuts, when we all hear a gun firin' and then y'all came along. Ain't that the truth.'

The cop glared at the old man. 'You speak when you're spoken to, boy. I was talking to these gentlemen.'

Before I could open my mouth, El Greco was backing up the old man, repeating his line and adding that he thought there was a man lying in the street down by the police car, but he couldn't be sure because we had not been down that way.

'I still don't know what in the hell you kids are doing round here. This is one dangerous part of town,' the cop said, shaking his head again. He was the kind of guy who liked to shake his head a lot, you could tell. He turned to the nut seller and said, 'You puttin' that on, or are you really blind?'

'No, suh, born blin' as a mouse, never seed the light o' day.'

'No point me asking you if you saw who blew that kid away, then.'

'No, suh.'

He could have asked the old man if he had heard anything, and then he might have learned something, but I guess the old man would have said he was deaf too. Nobody about. Nobody saw anything. Least of all not us.

'Where you kids from?'

'We're staying at Fat Chester's, sir, on our way to Savannah,'

'Guess I'll be taking you on out there, then. Crazy kids.' He shook his head again. Boy, he was some head-shaker.

A second police car arrived, all sirens and lights, and after an exchange of words our cop told us to get in his car and we started off for Fat Chester's.

The streets were empty as a fish lake on Friday.

– THIRTEEN –

We slipped out of Wilmington as the sun was getting up. Stiff from broken sleep and yawning heavily, we rode up through the suburbs, quiet as catacombs and grey with summer dust. White porch pillars glowed rose and bathroom lights shone, luminous against the brooding early light. My pop said we needed to get out of that town as quick as possible. 'Before you boys get yourselves killed,' as he put it, blunt as hell. Then he added, 'Lord knows what your mother would do to me if that happened. My life would not be worth two bucks.'

Obviously we must have been worth about a dollar each, maybe even fifty cents apiece.

We pushed down through the business district, passing buses filled with negroes on their way to clean towering glass parliaments, inside and out, polishing windows and tipping trash down chutes, claret bottles and Coke bottles banging dull and echoing like muffled gunfire through acres of space into dumpsters in basements the presidents and VPs and managers never saw. Fat women in print dresses and tennis shoes, clutching lunch boxes, calling to one another as they filed off the bus and into Howard Johnson's, Holiday Inn or some such places; to wash sheets and towels and dust the vanity tables of rooms they would never get to stay in, not even if they saved their bucks and had the price of the key.

Then we were up to the waterfront and suddenly over the Cape Fear River, view dissected by the criss-crossed spans of the steel bridge high above the toffee water. A tugboat, fat and stubby, funnel spewing black smoke that fell heavy in its wake, passed under the bridge and out of view. I turned in my seat to watch it reappear on the seaward side, then it was lost again as we hit the downslope and headed out past stoic warehouses that waited anxiously for precious cargoes from Europe and the Caribbean and Africa.

Scotch whisky. Sugar cane. Pineapples. Gold.

We stopped at the red light at the intersection of Mariette and Robert E. Lee where a late-night whore, skirt higher than a victory flag, asked my father for a light for her cigarette. He told a lie. Straight-faced with an apologetic smile, he said he was sorry but he didn't have a light, then he turned right on the red, even though he wanted to head straight.

'That young woman ought to be home sleeping.'

He adopted his minister's voice. My pop was a kind of amateur preacher, a sort of part-time minister. He read sermons and stuff every other Sunday at our church. Bill Bollbenden gave the other two. Bill Ballbender we called him. My father made the statement about the whore in the same tone he reserved for his sermons and for lectures to me.

El Greco and I damned nearly broke our necks turning round and trying to look up her skirt as she bent forward to ask the same question of the driver behind us, a bald-headed shoe salesman from Biloxi, who was driving a Mustang, top down.

My father turned left and left again through industrial units, where workshops had titles: Big Bob's Paint Shop; Wilmington Mailboxes; The Carolina Clutch Company. We hit the road we should have taken until the hooker embarrassed my father into turning off. He threw the old car right and we were back on track. To my relief he hit Interstate 17, straight on out to Winnabow in the county of Brunswick, through Bolivia; skirting Calabash, we crossed out of the Tar Heel and into the Palmetto State. South Carolina. My pop cracked on about some history concerning the Civil War, but my head was back outside the bar that never was, with blood spraying and thunder hammering through the night.

When the cop had taken us back to Fat Chester's, my pop had come running out through the screen door, frowning, looking like the fury of hell itself, assuming we had been picked up for some misdemeanour, or some such petty crime as throwing stones at warehouse windows.

El Greco and I had sat in the car, still and silent as woodcarvings, letting the cop do his bit. He huddled up close to my pop, hand on his shoulder, then they walked back closer to the squad car. I listened to his blurb.

'Mister Walsh, sir, them boys is lucky to be alive. Wanderin' around a place like that, could have gotten themselves killed easy as you like. Goddamned niggers runnin' around the place shooting like they was in a Wild West show. Thank the Lord it was just some nigger that got shot and not one of your boys. Lord knows what they were doin' over there in the first place. Said they were buyin' nuts. Beats me for sure. All the time there's been Haslams in this town, five generations, none of 'em ever went into that neighbour- hood, 'cept for me, and believe me that ain't by choice. And for sure I never knew no white folks who went there to buy nuts. Not even pecans.'

I had always wanted to ride in a police car. Put the siren on, flash the lights, chase bad guys. But all I wanted right then was to get out of his car, and see the back of Officer Haslam. If Lloyd had been that cop, he would have been knocking on doors, tracking the culprit, but this ol' boy wasn't Lloyd; this ol' boy had an agenda all his own. I couldn't even raise a smile when I thought of Lloyd, not even when I pictured the time just before Hallowe'en when El Greco and I tied firecrackers to the back of his patrol car while he sat drinking coffee outside the Roadway one starless night. Lloyd had leapt out of that car quicker than a frightened cat, gun waving, coffee all down the front of his uniform pants. Next he was pulling at his pants like a madman. The coffee from the Roadway was always hot as hell and we knew it through experience. His precious parts were on fire. El Greco and I were choking trying not to be heard, kneeling on the bench seat in the cab of Olsen's unlocked breakdown truck, with its legend, 'First for the Highway!' The two of us, staring out through the rear window, giggling like madmen at Lloyd who was dancing around trying to keep his soaked pants away from his blistering privates. God, that was funny.

Haslam came back to the car, waved us out and, shaking his head from side to side, said, 'Now you take good care of these boys, minister.'

He drove off slowly, down through the parking lot, spat out the window, then split the air with his siren, wailing and flashing off into the night. My father was clearly shaken by the story Haslam had told him, and, after holding us both so tight I thought my lungs would burst, he sent us to bed with cookies and milkshakes. I had vanilla, El Greco had peach, but neither of us touched them. He'd have been wiser to have given us a couple of Kents and a splash of Wild Turkey.

I think I caused my father to worry a lot in those days. He had never before allowed me to eat in bed, and certainly not in someone else's.

The Waccamaw River ran south out of its namesake lake for twenty-five miles, then, as though it feared the sea, or maybe because it preferred the land, where it had importance and a name, it turned southwest and ran parallel to the coast for sixty miles or so, until it turned sharp left at Georgetown and, tired from its journey, dumped a fat load of silt into Winyah Bay where it accumulated over the years and assumed a name: North Island.

We rolled easily down 17, sandwiched as it was between the Waccamaw and the ocean, along a shoestring of land known as the Grand Strand. Pine trees, golf courses and sand hills, sedge and Bermuda grass. Beautiful country with slashes of red soil the colour of rust where flash-flood tributaries had cut the earth in winter, but which were now dried hard and dusty. A clearing, trees cut and felled, silent tractors, and piles of bulldozed earth like so many termite hills lay waiting for the busy hands of men. Cattle, mute and gazing, stood lined up as though awaiting orders, oblivious as we rode by. A dozen hens behind them pecking the grass reminded me of the hobos in Central Park who scavenge the grass around Wolman Rink where picnickers have sat, looking for change and discarded cigarette butts.

Little River, Nixons Crossroads – a do-nothing hamlet that told of one man's destiny maybe – North Myrtle Beach, jealous little cousin of its famous relative, then Atlantic Beach, Windy Hill Beach, and finally the real deal, Myrtle Beach itself.

My pop must have reckoned we'd driven far enough away from dangerous Wilmington, for he pulled up by the boardwalk with a flourish, patted our heads, and just about yelled that he could eat a horse. El Greco and I had been quiet for most of our ride, content to stare at the country, thoughts flitting about the way that butter-flies rise in clouds from cornfields when harvesters scythe the ripened crop, flying random and seemingly aimless, but tight-bonded about some genetic purpose.

We ate a sour breakfast at Denny's. The food was fine, but we didn't eat much. My pop tried hard to gee us up, but his jokes fell flat as the pancakes. Even El Greco could not bring himself to smile more than a polite smirk when he said, 'I could eat a pony, Tony. Pass the cakes my way, J.J.'

I didn't blame him. He was doing the best he knew. It just wasn't working. We hadn't talked much about it, save for to say things about the size of that gun and ask each other what might have been the beef between the three men, and I could not imagine for an instant ever being in a situation where Cecil would shoot someone in a fight over me. El Greco remarked that I had more chance of being shot by Adolf than of him fighting my corner, to which I sadly had to agree. We were still haunted by the sound of gunfire and a scene of violence that had been burned deep within us, reinforced by the realisation that the racial hatred of Officer Haslam was open and undisguised, but just as deep-felt as Missus Felton's views, which caused me to worry that I wouldn't be able to look the same way at my elders and neighbours again.

It was still early, and people were active everywhere, rolling barrels into cellars, lifting boxes of salad and vegetables from off the back of flatbeds, fixing advertising bills in windows, lifting racks of sun oil on to sidewalks, setting up sunglass displays, filling magazine stands. Living life. Getting along.

I watched a man with one leg swing himself along the street, body suspended from tall wooden crutches tucked in each armpit, good leg swinging like a pendulum, timed perfectly to catch the floor as the sticks swung away and front again, pinned pant leg flapping in the soft breeze. He was licking along the sidewalk, fairly racing, and I asked myself where a man with one leg could be going in such a goddamned rush.

Maybe he was still running from whatever it was that took his leg.

He had on a T-shirt that said, 'Made in America. Finished in Vietnam.'

A skinny middle-aged pot-bellied man walking a no-brand dog stopped to let it crap by a post outside our window. The dog crouched down, straining and twitching its ass, oblivious to our gawping faces. Our server ran out into the street flapping a dishtowel, yelling at the guy, threatening to call the cops. Potbelly threatened to bring his dog inside and have it crap on the counter if he didn't just fly off back to Puerto Rico where, according to him, the waiter belonged. The waiter started yelling, 'Get Maurice! Get Maurice!' pronouncing it Mo-reece, so the guy shouted, 'Get who the fuck you want, you son-of-a-bitch!' He thought better of hanging around to check out Mo-reece though, so he dragged the immobile dog along by its leather leash, feet fixed and skidding, protesting at unfinished business. Just as well for him that he went when he did, for ten seconds later the maddest-looking Chinese guy I ever saw came rushing into the street armed with a meat cleaver, sharp as the President's suits. I had never heard of a Chinese having a name like Maurice before, and I thought about asking how he got his name, until I cast another look at that meat cleaver and decided I didn't want to know after all.

At least the meal had some interest. Good old American cabaret.

I didn't much care what happened around me, as long as something did. I was easily bored. Maybe that had something to do with how the fire we started near Green Valleys park began. I just didn't have the patience to sit out an event, to make sure it was a done deal, before I was off to the next. We sometimes got so bored we would climb up on the roof of Chang's food market, walk around the wall to the back yard and try to spear apples from the wood crates below, using a lock knife tied to a piece of string. It wasn't easy lifting an apple twelve feet in the air on a smooth bladed knife, but we would try it once or twice a month, until Chang Lee got tired of finding his apples stabbed to death all over the yard and fitted a plastic roof.

My father gave us each a couple of dollars, saying we could spend a half-hour on the rides across from Denny's while he called my mom and read his paper. He wanted to read the sports, see how the Mets were doing. My pop cared more about baseball than life itself.

There was a rollercoaster at Myrtle Beach, not a great big one like the giant dipper at Santa Cruz, California, a picture of which El Greco had on his bedroom wall, along with his collection of views of the Pacific Ocean: of Big Sur, Carmel, and whales in their dozens off the headland by Davenport. We decided to try that first, standing up in our seats with our arms raised as the wind rushed up at us, stomachs up by our teeth. It was over in seconds but when we came off, thinking of going round again, a sour-faced guy, purple drinker's face, Thunderbird breath, said, 'Can't you kids read? It says *Safety Notice. All Passengers Must Remain Seated.*'

Quick as a flash I raised my hands, expressing misunderstanding, and said, '*Je ne comprends pas,*' which was a

French expression I had learned by rote. It meant 'I do not understand'. It was brilliant. He stared at us, lost for words as El Greco compounded the act with a shrug of his shoulders.

As we walked off he said, loud enough for us to hear, 'Kids these days. All crap-ass wise-guys. Everyone's a comedian.'

I realised then this was the same guy we had bought the tickets from, who had asked if we had an adult with us, and to whom El Greco had said, 'No, sir, we're orphans.'

We made our way across to the ferris wheel, stuffed our pockets full of small pine cones from below a flat-topped tree and paid the spotty youth, who, trying to look tough as he took our money, nearly choked to death on a cigarette he was attempting to smoke to the filter without taking from his lips. We sat impatiently waiting for the wheel to turn, when suddenly, almost silently, it started to revolve, only the click of gears, growing fainter as we swung into the air, betraying the effort involved. Our chair rose up and out, the sense of freedom and sudden quiet enthralling as people fell away. The wheel revolved in a steady rush and we looked out far to sea, a pair of freighters on the horizon making their way to Wilmington, then inland where sat the lazy Waccamaw River and the tiny figures of golfers on the links between.

Then came our moment, when the wheel slowed to a stop, and we sat rolling gently back and forth so high above the ground. We started rocking our car, terrified but charged by the danger and neither of us willing to show it, the distant sound of the smoking kid calling to us not to move waved away on the breeze; then, tired of that, we sat still. After a minute, confident we were no longer being watched, we threw pine cones on to the boardwalk, and some on to the waltzers and merry-go-rounds now filling with kids.

The spotty kid started shouting again, and the wheel turned downwards. We came to rest. The angry youth, new cigarette lit and smoking hard, shouted at us to get off the ride. He told us to wait by the kiosk, that the owner had called the cops. We stood by the kiosk for ten seconds at most, then, without a signal but on our bond of understanding, we ran off through the swelling crowds of holidaymakers, to shouts from behind. We crossed the boardwalk and street, barely checking for danger as we ran between gleaming autos and delivery trucks, then we were round through the parking lot at the rear of the Gay Dolphin Gift Cove, down the alleyway leading around to Denny's, and in through the side door.

I told my father, who was drinking coffee, paper folded and held in front of him, that we were keen to hit the road, and that we'd wait in the car. He started to say that there was no rush, but we were gone. We kept low, watching for trouble, then we were in through the unlocked driver's door, over the bench seat, and squatting down in the well, waiting for my pop. He came shuffling along, paper still held up, desperate for sports. It was a wonder he wasn't knocked down as he drifted through the cars.

He placed his newspaper on the seat beside him, put the big car in reverse and, engine growling low and deep, pulled back out into the street. As he was about to move off, a cop arrived on a motor-cycle and pulled across the front of the old Buick. My heart stopped. El Greco glanced sharply at me, but the cop just set his kick-stand down in the space we had vacated and as he swung his leg over the frame my father pulled the car straight and, whistling 'Swanee River', headed for Georgetown, by way of Surfside Beach, Murrells Inlet and Pawleys Island.

We had escaped again.

Little puffs of cloud, white and billowy with the easy outline of boulders covered by fresh snow, hung in clusters in the otherwise peerless sky. I watched them from the open window, arms folded on the door rim, head laid to the side, wind rushing by. As if magnetic, they pulled together, piling higher and wider, deepening into the anvil shape of storm clouds, as though someone were emptying a spray gun into water. As quick as snakes their core turned grey, darkening again to gunmetal as we rode towards them along the spit.

Rain, in misty black rods, fell across the scene ahead of us, and moments later we were in the thick of it. A first few heavy drops against the hood and windshield, then in sheets as dense as Perspex across the glass, wiper blades whacking frenziedly, thumping and sucking to and fro. The old car sloshed through rivers of rainwater as we pulled into a truck stop.

'Boy, this is some storm.'

My father had a way with words. There was nothing we could say. He had said it all.

He picked up his paper and started in on the sports. I pulled a playing card of a naked lady from my wallet. Ricky Sullivan had stolen it from a pack his father had left in a bureau way back in the days when Ricky was too small to reach into and search the cabinet. But, since Ricky had gotten bigger and older and had found a thrill in the art of search, something that would eventually lead to juvenile hall and a career in office and house burglary, nothing in that household was safe. The woman had on white stockings, no bra and no panties. She had the bushiest thatch you ever saw, tastefully and artistically shaped into a love heart. I flashed the card to El Greco, who shook with laughter. He had seen the card before, many times, but each time I showed it to him he laughed fit to bust.

166

Naturally, the card was the Queen of Hearts.

The storm vanished as quickly as it arrived, heading north as it dissipated into space. The white-walls hissed on the wet roadway, spray whirling in our wake, whipped up through the treads. Steam rose off the asphalt and from the tarpaper roof of a cow byre abandoned on old farmland, now the ninth fairway of the Patterson Country Club. A dog barked unseen, somewhere off through a copse, chasing squirrels. A line of poplars, straight as a blade, led away from a farmhouse in the distance, marking the southern edge of a freshwater ditch that ran to a pond, bulrushes betraying its position, water hidden from view by mounds of grassy earth.

The air, thickened by water vapour, hung hot and heavy.

It was August 12th 1970, the day President Nixon signed the Postal Reorganization Act, giving the postal service the status of independent government corporation. It was announced on the radio news, to which my dad said, 'Wowee, that should change the world.' He was really waiting for the sports to come on so he could blow hot and cold about who he liked and who he didn't.

Something quite momentous had, however, changed the world the previous year. It really didn't have much to do with Nixon, who had scraped into the presidency on November 5th 1968, a few votes ahead of Hubert Humphrey, thanks to George Wallace, who took enough votes from Honest Hubert to let in Tricky Dicky. Some country, electing a burglar. Ricky Sullivan ought to have stood for office. This was the same Richard Milhous Nixon who, in November 1962, as former Republican vice president, was defeated in the California gubernatorial elections, had got all huffed up and announced his retirement from politics, stating, 'You won't have Nixon to kick around any more.' Some joker.

The momentous event had a lot more to do with LBJ, but it was really started by JFK, as it was he who put John H. Glenn Jr. into space: the first American. It seemed to me, listening to other people's conversations as I was wont to do, that all the others could manage – that was, the Russians and the Chinese – was to shoot dogs and monkeys at the stars. Whereas on July 20th 1969 Neil A. Armstrong and Colonel Edwin E. Aldrin Jr. had made unbelievable history.

'*Houston, Tranquillity Base here. The Eagle has landed.*'

Then good ol' Neil dropped his clogs down in the dust and uttered the immortal line, '*That's one small step for man, one giant leap for mankind.*'

The boys at Mission Control had gone berserk and El Greco and I had sat focused and rigid, resting on our elbows, fascinated and enthralled while my pop said things like, 'Whoever would have believed it? Not in my lifetime, that's for sure,' and one you could bank on from my old man: 'God must be on their side.' He came out with lots of stuff, often with God in it.

My mom had watched it too, saying, 'Isn't that wonderful, boys – who knows, maybe some day you'll go to the moon too.'

Adolf said I had already been there. He said I was lost in space most of the time, so the chances were that I already knew it well. Just like him. I bet my mom wished she could go to the moon. I bet she would have liked to have gone to Moon, Pennsylvania, just to get away from Oceanside, and the veneer of 'somewhere' that overcoated the mediocrity of that town. Pennsylvania was a great state – some of the best names in America. Blue Knob. Shy Beaver. Beavertown. Paradise. Cherrytown. Knobsville. Lovejoy. Cherry

Valley. New Beaver. Intercourse. Big Beaver. Even a mountain called King Knob. El Greco and I often went through the towns index of states to find the rudest names. Pennsylvania was number one.

Some time later Neil and Buzz had had a drive around the Sea of Tranquillity in a cart that looked as though it was made by someone down at Bubba's Gas Station. El Greco had tried to demonstrate to me just how far 238,000 miles was. He told me that as the crow flies it was near as dammit two and a half thousand miles from Oceanside to LA. Therefore going to the moon, even one way, was like going from here to there one hundred times. It was too much to think about. I had only ever watched crows flying in loops from the rookery in the elms by the courthouse, and they never seemed to go too far, never mind flying straight.

It seemed as though the world went mad for a few weeks. Everything was moon this and lunar that. Even ice-cream was Apollo Apple flavour.

Buzz Banana flavour. Nutty Neil flavour. Tutti-frutti Moondust flavour.

Michael Collins seemed to get overlooked in all the fuss, maybe because he didn't have a middle initial or the same name as his father. My pop said it was a truly amazing event, all the more poignant since it was exactly one hundred years since an expedition led by John Wesley Powell had completed the first passage of the Grand Canyon, and that these days people could fly over it in a six-seater Cessna for twenty bucks a throw from Boulder City airfield. And they even got to fly over the dam too.

Picasso said, 'I have no opinion about it, and I don't care.'

The Reverend Jesse Jackson said, 'How can this nation swell

and swagger with technological pride when it has a spiritual will so crippled?'

But perhaps the last word on the subject had been had by Mister Schwartz, who, carrying the Star-Spangled Banner in one hand together with a silver bugle, and drinking from a champagne bottle he held in the other, tooting and hollering all at the same time, yelled, 'The drinks are on me!' He had held an impromptu party at his house that lasted two days, and which my father finally stated was shameful, as Mister Schwartz had left the running of his store, single-handed, to his wife.

We stopped for gas one hundred miles south of Myrtle Beach, at the Texaco on Coleman Boulevard in Mount Pleasant, then we were across into elegant Charleston, spread like a chequered cloth over the Ashley and Cooper Rivers. My father rattled on about how the Civil War started in that city, at Fort Sumter on April 12th 1861. General Beauregard bombed the hell out of Major Anderson's fort, making the Unionist Anderson surrender in just one day. Anderson had been Beauregard's artillery instructor at West Point, and Beauregard had been his star pupil. He did a great job. Good teacher.

He must have been pretty pissed at the fact that he was only a major and his pupil was a general. Such is life. I wished I could have bombed the hell out of Mister Barr, and brought that man to his knees. Mister Barr was definitely not a great teacher. He foamed at the mouth and he spat when he spoke.

The Unionists got their own back when they retook the fort on Good Friday in 1865. It was Bad Friday for the rebels. It was too for Abraham Lincoln. It was the day he was assassinated.

My pop was like El Greco, full of facts. The difference was that Tony Papadakis couldn't have cared one single fuck about what happened to the Mets. I think I pretty much impressed my father when I pointed out that Joseph Pulitzer died in Charleston but was buried at Woodlawn. I never knew why they would have shipped him all the way to New York City. El Greco chirped in and said he died on his motor yacht in Charleston Harbour, on his way to Georgia, just like us. He must have been a bit off by the time they got him back to Woodlawn.

We ate lunch late, sitting outside Nice Al's sandwich bar on East Bay Street, shaded from the sun under the awning. Nice Al was okay. Not nice in the best sense of the word, but he was courteous and friendly enough in a reserved kind of way, what with his funny accent and all. His sandwiches were good though. I had ham, Emmental cheese and pineapple, with hot chilli sauce. El Greco had chicken with horseradish, onions and mustard. My father pulled a face, but Nice Al took the orders without batting an eyelid. My pop had salt beef. We drank gallons of soda, and two cups of black coffee.

Charleston was the prettiest town I ever saw. We marvelled at the wrought-iron balconies, like lace on a Spanish gown, perfect in their situation overhanging the shadowed streets, against red and bright orange brick or candy-coloured stucco in soft shades of mint and lemon and puce. Spanish moss as fine as gossamer suspended from branches of oily green; overhanging courtyards shaded for comfort and respite from the summer heat. White-painted iron chairs and terracotta tubs of begonias and lilies, iris and nasturtium. Bougainvillea, in clouds of purple and deep blood-red, frothing from arches over iron gates. The influence of Huguenots,

Arcadians and Creoles stamped everywhere. Splendid in its perfection.

And to think that my father had suggested driving us up to Cooperstown, New York State, to Doubleday Field and the Baseball Hall of Fame. We had missed out on a trip there the previous year because there was some fuss about hippies in their thousands heading up to some place called Woodstock for a pop concert which my father muttered was 'too dang close to Cooperstown' for his liking. The Hall of Fame was just fine, but we'd been there a thousand times, and, pretty though Cooperstown was, Charleston was something else. Even James Fenimore Cooper couldn't have argued with that. Even if his dad did build the town and name it after himself. 'Glimmerglass', he called it in some book. If Jimmy F. Cooper had been to Charleston, he'd have called it 'Superglimmerglass'.

I would have liked to stay in Charleston, perhaps forever. My mother said she loved that city, excepting that the people there thought they were a cut above everyone, and most of them would have reintroduced slavery if anyone ever gave them half a chance. My mother didn't much hold with the idea of slavery. I sometimes thought that maybe she felt she was enslaved herself. Chained to my pop, Cecil, Lauren and me.

I asked my pop if we could come back some day, maybe stay a week in one of the guesthouses on Broad or Meeting Street. He said, 'Sure,' which with him could mean anything. It could mean we'd be back next spring, or to celebrate my graduation, if I lived that long. I said it would be great to stop by Nice Al's for a sandwich too, if he was still in business. I suggested that it might be better for his business for Al to change his restaurant name to Pleasant-Enough Al's, laughing out loud when I said it. My pop,

172

who had sat at the counter talking to Al while El Greco and I sat outside, told me that the bar got its title from the fact that Al was French, from a town called Nice, which was pronounced like 'niece' as in 'niece and nephew' and was nothing to do with his personality.

I got into the car reluctantly, dragging my feet like a dog whose walk is nearing its end. The starter bit and the motor throbbed solidly under the hood, deep and strong as a ship's engine, then Pop put it into drive and we pulled away, sliding into the easy swell of traffic, and away from the town I newly loved.

We floated through the thick warm air, sailors on a tranquil sea, out through St Andrews to the Savannah Highway, and Johns Island. Antebellum plantation houses, glorious with neoclassical columns and arched glass windows glinting in the sunlight, passed behind us as we rode the highway south, the wealth of historic families like a thrust-out jaw in the middle of the landscape. Arrogant, and at the same time compelling and magnificent.

I loved the wacky way the people of Charleston spoke, everything drawn out and emphasised, as though the language was too rich to swallow, so that words must be savoured, rolled around the tongue like fine cognac, each syllable given time and consideration, not merely parts in communication but each one a work of art, valued for itself. El Greco and I practised speaking like Blanche DuBois. El Greco was brilliant and I wasn't half bad, if I do say so. We amused ourselves in this fashion as we drove along, the three of us spaced out on the big bench seat, my father smoking, flicking ash into the cigarette tray in the dashboard. We rolled through scenery as good as it gets, and everywhere signs of backbreaking enterprise, of cotton-pickers and share-croppers, children, barefoot and ragged, driving sheep and goats, seeking out fodder, thirsty dogs following. An old man, shirtless and ebony on the porch of a one-room house, tarred roof glistening like coal, played a guitar, the sounds of sevenths and minors ringing out on the air, melancholy and beautiful. I breathed heavily as I caught the scent of rosemary, fresh-cut and enticing, a child carrying a handful to her mother for the pot. And below it all an uneasy peace, where two worlds existed, one on top of the other, the way that a cat lies over its kittens.

Osborn, Parkers Ferry, Ashepoo. Name-boards only, and on through Gardens Corner, where we avoided running down a dog that sprinted out from a reed patch into our path, chasing mallards. My father braked hard, the heavy car sliding suddenly on the dusty road, and cursed under his breath. Although I could not make out his words for sure, I'm pretty certain he said, 'Damned fuckin' dog!' Which, if my mother ever heard him say it, would mean more trouble than he ever bargained for.

Lobeco, and then the outskirts of Beaufort, the second-oldest town in South Carolina. We shouted, 'Heya-look, they-as Beyoo-furd' and other such things in our mock Southern accents. I think my father was tiring of it, as he turned the transistor radio up loud, reaching over to flick the dial.

Beaufort was beautiful too. Rows of antebellum mansions lining the wide avenues, graced by trees of stature. Spanish moss hanging in veils put in mind mysterious women of the East, while perky Southern belles, all pretty as new snow, bounced along the sidewalks, coy and promissory. We diverted through the streets of Beaufort, 'Just to get a flavour of the place,' as my pop put it. I decided the South had more charm than the North ever had, and Tony said he wished the Confederates had won the war. We stopped for snow cones at a drugstore that had a sign in olde English script: 'Pinchman's Drugs and Confectionery'. I had peach Melba, El Greco had peach and apricot, and my father had plain peach. Everywhere you went in the South, you could get peach anything. Peach pie, peach ice-cream, peach juice, peach tart, peach meringue, peach cobbler. I bet most of those folks down there had peach piss, what with there being so much peach about.

We cut out of Beaufort, back to the 170: sweet blue Port Royal Sound half masked by Hilton Head Island in the distance. Then, as if by magic, we were on the great bridge over the Savannah River, glorious and sluggish green, and into the Peach State itself and then our goal, the town of Savannah.

All three of us cheered as the great sign 'Welcome to Savannah' loomed towards us. I had mixed feelings, and, as we quietened down, I knew El Greco did too. There is a sense of duality at the end of long journeys, of the ending of travel, and the re-establishing of values, together with a sense of loss, as though the prospect for adventure is all but gone, and mediocrity is its replacement. I worried about mediocrity. I worried that my mother worried about it too.

– FOURTEEN –

Savannah lay before us, lush and elegant, caught in time, preserved by luck and judgement, a great pearl thrown up seventeen miles from the ocean, as though too delicate to be cut and bruised by the sometimes angry sea.

Old Man Taylor once told me that some people, in fact most, spend the first part of their lives wishing they were twenty-one, and, once that event is over, they spend the rest of their lives wishing the same thing. Right to their graves.

He said people were hopeless dreamers, but that was their nature, and without that ability most of them couldn't cope with the hardships and the disappointments of life. I knew he was thinking of Joan, wishing they were twenty-one again, young and healthy and much in love.

Savannah was that dreamer, clinging to her past, her history, nailing her colours to her mast.

Coming off 17 through the wildlife refuge with its swamps and birds like spreadshot thick in the air, there is almost no moment like it, when rushing upwards, cloaked in mystery, comes the seducer, and the seductress, all in one.

If I was in love with Charleston, I was unfaithful with Savannah.

Like a high-breasted débutante, a Southern belle dancing in her satin gown, lace fan held across her scarlet lips, dark eyes flashing, hidden treasure promising to reveal, she drew us in.

Shades of green never before seen; blues, yellows, reds, indigo. Shades of the spectrum diffused and mixed by uninhibited artists; and white, brighter than snow, like the light in dreams. A city of hues, tints, tones. A city of the seven veils. Suspicious, moody, dark, mysterious. A city of nuance, of gradation and degradation, mute and yet poetic; a tease who, after so much hidden promise, might yet strip to nakedness.

Crossing the bridge, as if some divinity welcomed us, from the radio, 'Statesboro Blues'. Wailing guitars, and the gritty soul of Man expressed, at first protesting, blending then with jubilation. So like that city itself. Two halves and two worlds, 'love' and 'hate' tattooed across its knuckles, Mom and Pop, past and present, here and now, tomorrow and forever, Sav and Anna.

We sat silent, Tony Papadakis and I. My father made words which were whipped around the windshield and out through the open window, stolen by the city, by the keeper of secrets, the jealous half, wary of those who might seek to betray it by telling its stories and revealing its past. But simmering below that dark reserved veneer the city's generous, cheery, giving side: the ageing harlot who leans on balcony rails, bosom spilling out, smiling, beckoning. She was every bit as powerful, as conniving; a siren, seducing suitors and passers-by alike, leaving them dazed and breathless, desperate for more.

I watched, amazed by the complexity of streets as we drove along cobbled and oyster-shell roads, seemingly older than time itself. Along River Street, linked as it was by iron walkways and old stone stairs to the upper edge of the bluffs of Factors Walk and Bay Street, and through Warren Square with its dogwoods and magnolias and Spanish moss dripping, filtering the shimmering sun. Then Abercorn Street, to the Owens-Thomas House at No.124.

177

My pop made us promise to stay in the grounds as he paid our entry fees. He said to look around the house too, because it was a beautiful example of British Regency, probably the finest in America. He told us he'd spent many a happy hour there when, as a child, he'd visited his aunt. He had to meet with the realtor or somebody to do with his aunt's house, call my mom, and get us a place to stay. He said he would be an hour or so at most. We could do much damage in an hour, and he knew it. Our encounter with the gritty side of unacknowledged urban America, the side he knew existed but chose to ignore, had unnerved him. He was a worried man. He sounded worried, too. We were glad to be rid of him. We had spent long enough on best behaviour.

We promised as expected, and wandered into the house. It was huge, with great heavy shuttered windows. It was stuffy inside, though. Full of old chairs and beds too small for a good night's sleep. There were marble busts of old guys with curly wigs, and marble fireplaces; and some old buffer taking tourists around in whispering sighing groups kept rattling on about someone called Adam, who I took to be Adam from the Garden of Eden, but who El Greco told me was some old English architect guy. He read it on a plaque. Always reading. We looked at paintings of battles, which were neat: muskets firing plumes of smoke and orange flashes from their muzzles, drummer boys and flag-bearers, smoking cannons, and officers on horseback charging, swords in front of them; and always someone with lots of red and gold on a big white horse. When you've seen one battle painting you've seen them all, and we looked at millions of them. We got tired and went out to the garden.

It was mid-afternoon, and it was a boiler. Hot as a stripper's ass. We needed a smoke so we ducked out of sight, finding a shady hole between huge azaleas where we could sit unseen in the cool recess, but from where, through a gap in the shrubbery, we could see my father when he returned.

El Greco pulled the pack of Kents from out of his sock, a matchbook from the other, and, taking one, tossed the pack into my lap. I watched him idly as he lit his cigarette, then, as smoke drifted upwards in the still heat, he leaned across to light mine. Drawing heavily, grateful for the peace away from my pop and the prying eye of supervision, I exhaled slowly, smoke rolling out of my nose into the steamy air. El Greco laughed almost silently to himself, the way he often did. I laughed too, for no good reason, except that he was amused. We sat laughing to ourselves for what seemed like forever, until El Greco, tears rolling down his face, suddenly held his finger up to his lips, a signal to me to quieten down.

I froze, thinking my father had discovered us, until I heard the sound of a girl giggling. El Greco put his finger to his lips again and pointed to his right, indicating a gap in the clumps of dogwoods and azaleas. There, back of the thicket, was a young couple. He had his hand inside her blouse, all flowery and yellow with primroses. She was a looker, but demure in her long skirt and sneakers. Her hair was curly, and red as a rusty ship. We sat speechless, mesmerised. He was duff-looking, but he was doing great. She was rubbing his face and his hair, whispering, but loud, 'Oh, Dick! Oh, Dick!'

I didn't know whether she was referring to him or his anatomy, but I stared on, flushed in the face from excitement and the fear of being discovered. Lord knew what they did to peepers in the South. They tarred and feathered the negroes just for being black, so who knew what they would do if they caught someone ogling their women.

Then he did it, he pulled up her blouse, and slid her brassière up, and out came her titties, milk-white with rose-pink nipples. I nudged El Greco in my excitement, and he shoved me as a sign for me to sit still. Old Dick was rubbing her boobies like a man possessed and she was moaning and squirming. Then she turned her body side on to his and he lifted up her skirt, high up around her waist. She had on little white cotton panties, and the next second, just as she said, 'No, Dick, not here,' he pulled them down with one swift tug, and there, in its glory, was her bush, copper as a new church roof. I whistled. I couldn't help myself, it just came out. The next thing there was a scene of panic, her pulling her panties up, her brassière down, and tucking her shirt into her skirt in one practised motion. She shook her hair into place and before he had time to react she was down through the shrubbery and out on to the lawn. Dick was looking around venomously, but he couldn't see us, hidden as we were by shade and foliage. Then he was gone too, chasing after her, trying not to appear rushed, as he called out, 'Hayley! Hayley!' His shoes squeaked as he marched across the lawn.

I thought El Greco would be mad at me. 'I'm sorry, I just couldn't help myself.'

'To tell the truth, J.J., you beat me to it. Did you see her bush?'

'Sure did. Looked like Missus Schwartz's cat!'

'Sure did! Wowee! Hot damn! I'd give anything to see that again!'

'Me too. Some beaver. Nice-looking, too.'

'Which? The girl or the beaver?'

'Both!'

We laughed fit to bust.

We smoked another cigarette apiece, as the others had burned away without our noticing, then headed back out on to the lawns, still smirking.

They had a little stand selling ice-cream and suchlike, so we bought sodas and wandered aimlessly, waiting for my father. We passed Copper Bush and Dick, walking casually arm in arm behind her parents. We giggled hysterically as we passed, receiving bemused glances from Hayley's mother and father, and an angry look from Dick, who guessed rightly who the whistlers were. Hayley blushed as red as her hair, and we waltzed on, shaking with mirth as El Greco said, loud enough to be heard, 'Do you think she takes after her mom?'

Hayley's mother had hair the colour of carrots.

'Couldn't say for sure,' I laughed.

'I never saw her momma's bush!'

We exploded again but, afraid of Dick, who had turned towards us with a murderous look in his eyes, we ran across the lawn, spilling soda as we went. We sat in the shade of a cedar, below its fan-shaped limbs, peaceful now, as birdsong floated around the even chatter of people talking.

El Greco saw my pop first, standing by the back of the house, shielding his eyes like Captain Ahab. El Greco waved, and, seeing us, Pop waved back, then beckoned us to join him on the terrace. We sauntered across the lawn, the heat too much for more than gentle movement. He asked if we had a good time and El Greco, sharp as ever replied, 'Yes, sir. It was a sight to behold, quite edu-cational.'

My father smiled, relieved and satisfied. 'I knew you'd enjoy it here,' he said beaming. 'I always did.'

'Oh, I bet you never had as good a time as we did, Pop.'

181

'No, sir, I sure bet you did not,' said El Greco, turning away to make our secret sign.

My pop drove us around to the Olde Parsonage Guesthouse, right on the angle of West Hull Street and Chippewa Square. The owner was a blood-faced old guy in a check shirt and zip-up sweater. It was ninety degrees in the shade and humid as a tart's knickers but there he was, large as life, trussed up like a Thanksgiving turkey. He must have been waiting for us, standing outside this great old house: red brick, white shutters, dark green gables, dark green door, giant brass letterbox and brass lion-head knocker the size of a catcher's mitt. We climbed out from the Buick, and he shook our hands, each of us in turn starting with El Greco and finishing with my pop.

'James Ellory,' he said, 'at your service. Welcome aboard.'

I couldn't resist it, so I said, 'J.J. Walsh. Pleased to make your acquaintance, sir. Kind of chilly for August, ain't it?'

He guffawed in a slow kind of way, all rich and deep and honeyed, like a pipe-smoker's cough. 'Pleased to meet you, J.J.' As if to emphasise the point he shook my hand a second time, and gave me a snappy salute, like Humphrey Bogart in *To Have and Have Not*.

We took our bags up to our room. Once inside the great marble-floored hallway I understood why he was dressed as he was. The downstairs of that old house was cold as a polar bear's ass.

'Air-conditioning,' he said simply. 'Missus Ellory hates August in Savannah. She calls it the month of the three aitches. Heat, humidity and heart attacks is how she puts it. I'll probably die from frostbite.' He chuckled to himself, and said, 'Follow me, shipmates.'

We made our way up the wide, curving staircase, and, as he

182

swung open the door to a room off the landing, heat bowled over us like breakers on a beach. He ushered us inside, and closed the door. 'Only two rules on board, boys. First, always close the doors. Second, Missus Ellory is always right.'

He went on to tell us that Missus Ellory was a direct descendant of Robert E. Lee and that strong blood ran in her family. He told us too about how he had been a sea captain, been most places in the world one time or another, and hinted at mysteries long since hidden away.

He was a liar, though. Missus Ellory told us he was a banker and the only sailing he ever did was up the coast to Daufuskie Island, or south to Ossabaw. He was a neat old guy, though. He told us stories about shipwrecks and mutinies, and days in the crow's nest, dying of thirst, surrounded by water and not a drop to drink, spying out land. I think he stole the bit about no drops to drink from *Robinson Crusoe* or *Treasure Island* or some such book, but he was fun. He was the kind of guy every kid should have for a grandpa. We listened as though we were spellbound, even though we didn't believe a word. He was a little like Mister Felton, who loved to tell kids stories. If you liked a story Mister Felton told, you could always buy it in his store.

My pop took us to the house where the garden killed his aunt. It was a great big rambling house, timber-clad, and designed as if by someone who drank while he planned, add-ons being the premise rather than an afterthought. It was a neat old house, though, and the garden, rich and prosperous in colours as though some madman had scythed his way through a paint store allowing spilled paint to flow untrammelled by thought or design or order, was testament that my great-aunt had not laboured in vain. Even the burglar probably admired her garden, right before he stole her silverware.

I never saw such a profusion of flowers, such richness of colour. My father said he just bet the old girl was sitting up on the roof ridge, looking down at us and her garden with pride. As if to prove his point he took off his hat and waved it slowly, holding it high above his head as he stared up at the slates. He smiled to himself, and, putting his hat back on, headed up the path, opened the screen, knocked loudly on the door, knocked again, and walked right in, as though he owned the place, which in truth he did. The tenants were all girl students, one of whom was called Randy, and I'll just bet she was. She had on shorts so tight she had us gawping from the second we followed my father inside, until he coughed theatrically to break our spell and I flushed red as a flare, the way I did when Missus Papadakis caught me staring at her, and we sought escape in the killer garden. Pop sorted out their complaints, which were few and minor I suspect, for they probably loved that house too, then we strolled back to the old Buick, waving like film stars to the girls who were standing in a line outside the door.

As we were staying just that night and starting back to Oceanside the very next morning, my pop drove us on out to Fort McAllister, by way of Richmond Hill, then around again in a loop through Savannah and out to Tybee Island, where, although it was late afternoon and the shadows were long, the heat pulsed around us, swaying the air. I guessed my pop had done the same kind of things with his pop, as he became lost and contemplative walking along the beach.

El Greco watched my father, sizing him up as we strolled.

'What you thinking about, Mister Walsh?'

'Oh, just times long gone, I guess, Tony.'

He hesitated, and added, 'I think sometimes we never fully see a picture until it's gone, and then all we have is photographs to remind us and, given time, we even forget to look at those.'

He was thinking of his own father. I knew. I knew because he leaned down and kissed the side of my head, pulling me close into him, as he had back in Wilmington, when we had rocked his world and his certainty, by wandering into the wrong place at the wrong time, curious in our innocence. I pulled a face at El Greco and, pulling myself free, raced down to the water, El Greco's feet hammering the hot sand behind me. We stopped at the water's edge. We couldn't strip off and swim, as El Greco had the pack of Kents inside his sock and I had the matchbook inside mine, so we contented ourselves with hurling stones into the sea, and watching yachts, white-hulled and white-sailed, heading up to Hilton Head and Port Royal.

We often watched yachts off the coast of Oceanside in summer, but never in numbers so great. There was something graceful in their silence, and only occasionally did one come close enough for us to hear the flap of sails. Watching them out on the deep blue of the sea made the horizon a mirror edge, white gulls against a blue sky their reflected image. We stood staring, taking in a scene worthy of the day, until my father, sensing our need, drove us back to the Ellory house, from where we walked around Savannah's old quarter, marvelling at the beauty of that fabulous town, where every store was richer-looking than its Oceanside counterpart, and altogether more mysterious and enticing; for they were new to us, and anything new was a pull we could not resist. Every place we passed that had a distant cousin in Oceanside was grander, and somehow seductive. Mae's Diner was eclipsed by every café we passed, the scent of French vanilla permeating the air, and odours of chocolate and hazelnut catching our imagination, so that we had to try them, much to my father's relief, as he could buy yet another paper and read the sports. The store we stopped by for a sports paper was a distant cousin of Mister Schwartz's store. It had foreign newspaper titles that Mister Schwartz had no demand for: *Le Monde*, *ABC*, *Der Spiegel*. Tony Papadakis was fascinated. He couldn't read French other than the few sentences we learned in school, or Spanish or German, but he looked through every one of those papers while my father was flicking through *Sports Illustrated*. My father settled on some baseball special magazine and we headed into the Lookout Café for French vanilla roast, black, no sugar. The pretty waitress gave us both a smile and winked at us when we ordered, and we grinned back, looking her up and down while my father read through the drinks card. He ordered a Coors malt beer, and got settled into his seat to read more stuff about baseball, most of which I guess he already knew. I'd kept my set of baseball cards Adolf had got me that birthday two years back, and I swear there were times, when I looked through those cards, when I felt a creeping affection for him. Then he would do some shit like punch me in the nose that took me right back to step one.

I guess my father figured we were growing up, because, instead of Denny's or some burger joint that we would normally beam into, he looked kind of mischievous and said, 'Boys, tonight we're going to live a little. I'm taking you to the restaurant I took Bryony to on our honeymoon. Probably still the best in all Savannah.' El Greco looked at me, kind of surprised that he had used my mom's name instead of calling her Missus Walsh. I suspected he was trying to make the end of the trip special to take our minds off of seeing a man's brains blown out; although he didn't know that, he just knew we had been around death and guns and bigotry, and when all else was done he was scared as all hell that my mom would nail him to a cross for ever letting us wander away into the evening in a strange town, while he talked baseball and religion and politics and the future of the Union with Fat Chester over a few pints of Miller.

We shrugged and said, 'Sure,' and his face lit up with delight. He couldn't have looked happier if he'd just heard Gil Hodges' Mets had beaten the Pittsburgh Pirates.

I offered to return to the Ellory house to brush my hair and smarten myself up, but my pop, in his new super-magnanimous role, said, 'What the hell, I'm a patron!'

This was so unlike him that I started to worry that the pretty waitress had given him bourbon instead of beer, but we rolled on down to the waterfront, and rocked right up to the door of Maison Philippe. This was swanky. Oceanside had nothing like this, and, even being fair to New Jersey, you would have had to skip the state and head to Manhattan to find a restaurant like this. We sat in chairs the size of canyons looking at menus in French, which fortunately had the real deal in tiny English lettering below. Not a burger in sight. El Greco pointed out stuff we had never seen before and we both screwed up our faces when we saw snails on the menu. What sort of person ate snails? Some people!

My father ordered garlic bread for us to share, and sea bass for himself. El Greco had chicken, and I had chicken too. We knew better than to order something we'd never heard of. All said and done it made my father happy, but I'd have taken Ricky Sullivan's father's ribs, or Tony's mom's barbecued chicken, any day.

We strolled back towards the Olde Parsonage Guesthouse under a moonlit sky, a slight haze from the heated sea misting the stars, but a beautiful night to fix images to remember Savannah by. At the corner of Bull Street and Johnson Square my father steered us across the street unexpectedly, then we saw the cause. Two gorgeous whores leaving little to the imagination standing in a bookshop doorway. If that had been Missus Felton's bookstore, no doubt she would have added prostitutes to her list of hates. I wondered if she would place them above or below coloureds in her hate-list pecking order. El Greco and I nearly broke our necks straining to get a better view as my father tried to distract our attention by pointing out Christ Church with its imposing columns and architectural grandeur, and reading out a bunch of facts about this being the third church on this site as the others burned down, and about some woman being the first negro to be baptised in Savannah, back on July 7th 1750. And all the time, as he read out facts, we strained to watch the hookers leaning forward, laughing and smiling, and waving at men in passing cars, showing tantalising moons of breast. My pop was right. We were growing up. Maybe Pan Am should have added an entry on page 210 of *New Horizons* under the heading 'Spectator Sports', after the Savannah Athletics baseball team: good-looking whores on the corner of Bull Street and Johnson Square. Now that would have put some extra interest into our favourite guide.

Cap'n James Ellory was sitting under a spreading live oak, Spanish moss draped and beautiful in the moonlight, smoking his pipe, his heavy cardigan draped over the back of a chair. He was sipping from a large glass of red wine, so I said, 'Thought you'd be havin' a tot o' rum, cap'n?'

Mister Ellory laughed his raspy laugh, fit to bust. 'You'll be first in the crow's nest on me next voyage, me hearty. Eyes like an eagle you've got there, me boy!'

He loved playing that role. I could see why Missus Ellory didn't want him to drop dead from a heart attack. He really was a neat old guy.

We passed through the arctic chill of Missus Ellory's refrigerated ground floor, and up to the heat above, receiving a bear hug each from my father before going into our room, its windows wide, where I slept disturbed, fitful sleep, punctuated by colossal bangs which jerked me bolt upright, gasping, clawing, pulling brains out of my mouth so I didn't choke, and desperately wiping blood from my eyes.

Next morning I awoke to find El Greco sitting on the edge of my bed, sunlight streaming through the open windows. He grinned at me and patted my head softly.

'Just dreams,' was all he said.

After breakfast we said our thanks and waved goodbye to Missus Ellory and the captain, cruising slowly off along West Hull Street, before heading up past the Harper Fowlkes House and Orleans Square, following signs for the Amtrak station and the i95.

There was something sad for El Greco and me about leaving the Forest City with all of its elegance and attractions, to replace it with the rock-steady certainties of Oceanside, of schooldays and routine. Questions flitted through my mind as we drove on out towards the highway, about some of the hidden secrets of our little town. For my own peace of mind I dismissed them as unanswer-able questions that only time would answer. It seemed that time was our friend on the one hand, bringing relief from hard times seen, but that, as time moved on, it brought with it new hardships, and things to bear. I thought about it some more, and recognised that time also brought joys and excitement, and the future whose prospect I so relished. I contented myself with the thought that whatever will be will be. El Greco had more than once told me that was the nature of life, that it was uncertain and full of surprises, some good, some not so good, and that we had to weigh them all and deal with them as we found them to be, without pre-judging. He said that people like his old man, who thought they knew everything, were full of shit.

I guess my pop was wise to miss out Wilmington on the way back, although I'm sure he would have liked to chew the cud with Fat Chester one more time. He chose routes and places to stay that avoided opportunities for us to veer off. Safe destinations, and guesthouses where he could keep us close. It struck me that, apart from leaving us at the Owens-Thomas House, where he figured we could do no harm, my father had chaperoned us every step of the way since Wilmington and our encounter with what had previously been very much the hidden truth of America. My thoughts still tumbled with images the like of which I had never seen, and, as we rolled into countryside away from Savannah, I saw shoeless children again in the cotton hamlets and tarpaper shacks. It dawned on me that these were children whose parents walked barefoot too. Poor people. People who could not afford everyday shoes. People who had just one pair of shoes. For church on Sunday. And there was me, wearing out shoes every few months, and my mother taking me to town to buy new ones, no question about it.

We were desperate for time alone, to smoke a cigarette and talk shit and tell crude jokes. Every time we suggested going for a mealtime walk or a leg-stretching stroll when we stopped for gas or coffee, my father immediately piped up that he fancied a walk too. He was starting to get on our nerves.

We learned something about return journeys though, about the end of adventure and its replacement by the mundanity of everyday life. It kind of made sense too. I often craved something special, something way too much, such as apple pie with honey and thick cream. The first spoonful in my mouth was like nothing I had tasted before, it was the most exquisite thing in the world for a few sweet seconds, but every subsequent spoonful was less rewarding than the one before, to a point where I had had too much of a good thing and dropped the remainder in the trash. It wasn't that the scenery was any different, or the sky less blue, but the sounds of the earth calling were muted. I guess we both sensed that, and contented ourselves with staring at the passing landscape, lost in thought, listening to the radio, trying to forget.

I lost track of where we were, neither of us poring over the Texaco and Philips road maps we had studied on the way down. My father pulled into a smart-looking diner on the edge of some nameless town just off 95. No scenic diversions on our return, just my father trying to get us home in one piece. To unload his burden of responsibility.

This place had great burgers, and not a snail in sight. When my father went to the john, I stared straight at El Greco. I worried that the sound of gunfire hammering across that fateful evening would never leave me, and that the bareness of race and its former irrelevance to me had been changed so that my innocence was not recoverable. I spent time on thoughts that had never troubled me before, and, when El Greco asked me what I was thinking about, I know he already knew and had his answer ready. I told him. He told me what he had told me before: that life is just a series of experiences, some big, some small, but that time was the one thing that would finally be our friend. He said that, just as we had witnessed Bobby learn to laugh again, and smile at funny memories of bowling ball Lester, so would we relax about that dreadful scene.

I looked him in the eye and asked, 'Was this my test?'

He looked at me for what seemed like forever, then smiled his dreamy smile, and said, 'No. Your test will come, and I guess so will mine. This is just a page in our book of life. You'll forget this soon, we both will. But fuck me, that was some gun.' He grinned at me then, teeth gleaming against his suntanned skin, as he shook his head from side to side, and did his wise old man thing. I felt comfort then. Tony Papadakis was a sage. He was thirteen years old.

My father came whistling out of the john and paid at the counter. He must have left a big tip because I heard the blousy waitress say, 'Why, thank you, honey, that is right kind of you.' My pop flushed, and raised a hand as if to say, 'Think nothing of it, I'm a generous guy.' He wouldn't have tipped that busty woman half so generously if my mom had been around.

As we walked out to the car, a thought rushed into my mind, then rushed out again in words.

'Pop. Some time, can we invite Tony and his mom and Katherine?' I paused momentarily before adding, 'And the Johnsons and their kids? For Thanksgiving maybe?'

My father stopped dead in his tracks, as did El Greco. He looked at me quizzically, then, after pursing his lips some, said, 'Sure. Why not? Your mother would like that. Forest Johnson can advise me on my insurance. Always good to have the old insurance in order.' He smacked me on top of the head with his newspaper, then ruffled my hair and El Greco's, before sliding into the big old car, lighting a Kent and pointing the fender north. I felt somewhat relieved, as though my worries were lessened, for reasons I couldn't define.

After two long days of mostly quiet travel, as uneventful as our journey down had been filled with anticipation and drama, we rolled back into Oceanside just before four o'clock. We passed Bobby walking with his mother and Mister Lincoln. My father tooted the car horn. We all waved, and I gave Bobby a big thumbs-up, as I had that time which seemed so long ago in church.

I asked my father to let us out by the cannery, and, relieved as all hell that we were back on safe ground, he said, 'Back by six.'

We waited for the old Buick to roll out of view, then made our way to our hole in the fence and headed out to the loading bay. Home again.

We sat on an old block crane weight and I looked up at the gulls, wheeling and clattering above us, as though they had been awaiting our return. El Greco passed me the pack of Kents. They were a little crunched from being crammed down his sock, so I straightened one, lit it, and handed it to him, then lit one for myself.

El Greco was staring hard; smoke floating around him, lost in his own thoughts, reminding me of my father looking out across Tybee Island.

'You can fit this baby twice into the mighty Pacific, and still get change.'

The mighty Pacific. That was how it was with El Greco. Every other sea was a poor relation.

'Seventy point eight per cent of this world is sea. You could live all your life on a boat – fish, and go up river and pull up drinking water in buckets, and net fallen fruit and driftwood – and never touch land. Think of that. You could even be buried at sea. Think of that.'

He got dreamy then, absent and lost in his world where only he went, the way my mother sometimes did. I knew that his need to see that ocean was something great, something deep within him, something intangible, more than merely an escape from the memory of his father and the fractured present that man had created for his mother, his sister, his grandfather and him.

For a fleeting moment the bitter turn of mouth, then an embarrassed shrug, the old El Greco grin, and we were one again.

Sensing that the adventure of our journey was at its end, and that our return to our homes and families had been swift and uneventful like most return journeys, and that this special time would soon be that thing my father had so recently referred to as a picture we fail to see, then in time a fading memory, I sought some future purpose to keep us bonded and hopeful.

'Some day we'll see it,' I said, nodding my head. 'Some day.'

'Some day soon, do you think?' he asked, squinting up against the sun.

'Some day soon,' I promised quietly. 'Some day soon.'

– FIFTEEN –

El Greco died two days past Thanksgiving. A great storm brewed over the Atlantic Ocean, clouds so black they turned day to night. White tops cresting on immense swollen waves, stark as neon against the inky sky, and the pulse of the world beating deep beneath the ocean, all too terrible to see. That storm swept in, and, as it came, fear rose like blood in every man, and Oceanside feared for its very existence, as though great sorrow itself was delivering fury on that community for failing that little boy. And I willed it in too. I willed it to smash the boats to matchwood, to throw the bobbing buoys from the water, to hurl them through the church, to uproot the trees and use them as bats against the courthouse, and for fire to sweep through there, engulfing the public library, then leaping to Mister Felton's old bookstore, reducing all to smoking ash. I wished the cannery would break into a million pieces and scythe through that town like shrapnel, wreaking havoc and terrible justice through the hospital in Cedar Hills, then on out to the farm belt, and on again through Lakewood and New Egypt, spiralling out through Trenton, Philadelphia, Salt Lake City, Reno, and on again to San Francisco, where, still furious, it would rip into the mighty Pacific and tear at the heart of that ocean for never being there, for only ever being a picture on a wall.

That illness came back to El Greco like that dreadful storm, suddenly, from out of a clear blue sky. One second it seemed there was Tony Papadakis and the very next there was aching loneliness – the loneliness created out of a child stolen from life itself, and the memory of a smile, the image of that boy who, if spared, had so much life to live.

His light faded the way a candle all burned down to its base fades, finding no more wick to burn as though the oxygen is all but gone, and with feeble little flickers it runs in on itself and suddenly all light is gone, with only a spiral of smoke as testimony to its ever having been.

The ice cube is long since gone, lost in a power failure that flooded Old Man Taylor's kitchen, proving that nothing is forever.

I often – hell, almost every day still – sit with that great old moose out on his peeling porch, the two of us staring out to space.

Looking for those we loved.

Epilogue

The old cannery still stands silent. Deepening rust on its great cranes, a little more paint peeled from them to exaggerate their scars, and from its soup-green corrugated shell, exposing the tin beneath. I sit there often, smoking Kents out on the loading bay, unseen save for the clattering seagulls and El Greco, who most days looks down on me from the clouds, or from the light-topped buoy, or the stern of a passing freighter. Sometimes I cry for his loss, afraid for myself and for him, but mostly now I return our secret sign, keeping alive what I can.

Acknowledgements

With thanks to Beryl Bainbridge, Carol Smith, Debbie McCabe, Wendy Loveday, N.E. David, Susan Bettinson-Thompson, Angela Toogood, Kay Reader, Paula Chandler, Al Duncan, Patrick Ravenscroft, Ian McKay, Paul Clerkin, Steve Rubie, Sharon Evans, Nick Smith, Brian Ferris, Bernabe Garcia, Damaris Bowker, José Angel Aznal Almargo, John Wiltshire, Peter Huggins, Robert Bohner-Eismann, Graham Collier, Dawn Preston, Alison Pybus, Sue Maguire, John Thornton, Joan Tildesley, Charles Measures, Ana Ammann, John Morgan, Penny Royle, Doug Palfreeman, Charles Obranowicz, Nigel Campbell, Deborah Ann Pascoe, Steve Evans, Martyn Alderdice, Amoun Mosharrafa, Lucy Ford, Helen Horsley, Christine Dalkin, Lawrence Edward Archer, Andrew Horsley, Diana Lyons, Niall Cox, Julian Greenwell, Archie Campbell, Heather Terry, Jeff Rutherford, Clive Thompson, Peter Preece, Jane Munro, Linda Oxberry-Baynes, Janet Philpot, Sushma Pugalia, Rosalyn Thompson, Helen Elliott, Trevor-Frank Quartermaine, Helen Minton, Lisa Kilcar, Ken Robinson, Philip Bage, Hugh McGouran, Gill Barratt, John Dawson, Maxine Findlay, Neil Batham, Nick Redfern, Kimberley Overfield, Raimundo Fernandez-Cuesta-Laborde, Olly Figg, Richard Green, Claire Vassallo, Linda Jessup, Charlotte Ward, Des Noble, Andy Parker, David George, Keith Bemrose, Jens Laursen-Schmidt, and

Anthony 'Hank' Lindo – variously for critique, advice, inspiration, support, challenge, belief and encouragement.

To Anna Burtt, Clare Christian and Heather Boisseau for believing in me, and making me believe that all things are possible. Thank you so much – I am indebted to you all – such truly wonderful ladies.

On the subject of wonderful ladies I would like to once again celebrate the amazing achievement of Yorkshire Rows in crossing the Atlantic Ocean in a rowing boat and setting a world record – thanks for inspiring us all – Janette Benaddi, Helen Butters, Frances Davies and Niki Doeg. Some day the mighty Pacific?

About the Author

Mark Thompson was raised in Stockton-on-Tees, England, and spent many years living in London before moving to Andalucia in southern Spain. He has travelled extensively throughout the United States over many years, harvesting material for writing both literature and songs. He plays guitar in a rock band, and now lives happily in the wilds of North Yorkshire with his partner Liz and three children.